Dead Water

(Kiera Hudson Series Two)
Book 6

Tim O'Rourke

ISBN: 10: 1483963187
ISBN-13: 978-1483963181

Story Editor (Hacker)
Lynda O'Rourke
Book cover designed by:
Carles Barrios
Copyright: Carles Barrios 2012
Copyedited by:
Carolyn M. Pinard
www.thesupernaturalbookeditor.com

This book is dedicated to

Gayle Morell

Thanks to:

Shana at bookvacations.wordpress.com
Braine & Cimmaron at Talkingsupe.com
Nikki Archer at vampsandstuff.com
Bella at paranormal book club
Suemcg-delirium.blogspot.com
Caroline Barker at Areadersreviewblog.wordpress.com
Who all took the time to review my books – Thank you!

You can contact Tim O'Rourke at

www.kierahudson.com

Or by email at Kierahudson91@aol.com

More books by Tim O'Rourke

Kiera Hudson Series

Vampire Shift (Kiera Hudson Series 1) Book 1
Vampire Wake (Kiera Hudson Series 1) Book 2
Vampire Hunt (Kiera Hudson Series 1) Book 3
Vampire Breed (Kiera Hudson Series 1) Book 4
Wolf House (Kiera Hudson Series 1) Book 4.5
Vampire Hollows (Kiera Hudson Series 1) Book 5
Dead Flesh (Kiera Hudson Series 2) Book 1
Dead Night (Kiera Hudson Series 2) Book 1.5
Dead Angels (Kiera Hudson Series 2) Book 2
Dead Statues (Kiera Hudson Series 2) Book 3
Dead Seth (Kiera Hudson Series 2) Book 4
Dead Wolf (Kiera Hudson Series 2) Book 5
Dead Water (Kiera Hudson Series 2) Book 6

Black Hill Farm (Books 1 & 2)
Black Hill Farm (Book 1)
Black Hill Farm: Andy's Diary (Book 2)

Sydney Hart Novels
Witch (A Sydney Hart Novel) Book 1
Yellow (A Sydney Hart Novel) Book 2

The Doorways Trilogy
Doorways (Doorways Trilogy Book 1)
The League of Doorways (Doorways Trilogy Book 2)

Moon Trilogy
Moonlight (Moon Trilogy) Book 1

Samantha Carter – Vampire Seeker Series
Vampire Seeker (Samantha Carter Series) Book 1

You can contact Tim O'Rourke at
www.kierahudson.com or by email at kierahudson91@aol.com

Chapter One

Kiera

Potter had wanted to talk, but I had nothing to say. Well, that wasn't entirely true – I had plenty I wanted to say to him. First, I wanted to get my thoughts straight. I needed to know each word that was going to trip off the end of my tongue; like placing one foot in front of the other. I didn't want Potter to jump in – make his excuses – before I'd had the chance to say what I wanted to.

As I stood in the vacant bedroom, peering through the dirty window and down the hill, Potter paced the wooden floorboards behind me. I glanced to my right and spied the pool of black blood my father had left behind on the floor. In the colourless morning sun, I could see the blood had dried into the shape of a butterfly. It looked like one of those pictures kids did in year-one at school, where they folded over the sheet of paper, squashing the thick globules of paint and spreading it flat to make some abstract pattern. I looked back out of the window. Murphy was making his way back up the hill. He trudged through the snow, which covered his police trousers almost to the knee. I watched silently as he came towards the cottage, and his hands looked red as if covered in blood. I looked harder and could see that they weren't covered in blood, but instead were red-raw with cold where he had dug his brother's – my father's – grave. Murphy's silver hair flopped over his brow and sparkled in the morning light. He looked tired. His face was drawn, thick, deep lines cut across it. The wrinkles gave the appearance that his face had cracked – turned to stone. I looked down and could see a mass of tiny cracks covering the backs of my hands. Potter must have caught me looking at them, as he came up beside me and took my hands in his.

I looked into his face. The bruises around his eyes, mouth, and jawline had started to fade. They now looked like yellow and green shadows. His nose looked bent out of shape, but then again, it had always looked broken; it's what gave his face that rugged, thuggish look. Holding my hands in his, he stared at me with his jet-black eyes.

"Talk to me, Kiera," he whispered.

"I have nothing to say to you," I said, easing my hands free of his and looking back out of the window.

"You can't ignore me forever," Potter said.

"I'm not ignoring you," I said, watching Murphy reach the police van which was parked outside. With his raw-looking hands, he clawed the snow from the windshield. "I'm angry with you. You lied to me..."

"I know you're angry with me," Potter said, "But you still need me."

"Need you?" I gasped, wheeling around on him. "I don't need you for anything."

Potter glanced down at my hands, then back at me. "Your flesh is starting to turn to stone again. You can feed on me if you want," he said, loosening the collar of his dark coat and exposing his neck.

"I'd rather feed on a skinwalker," I snapped, pushing past him.

"It might come to that if you're not prepared to feed off me," Potter said. "We're right out of the red stuff – Lot-13."

I shot a look at him, my innards starting to ache again. Slowly, I crossed the room, coming to rest inches from Potter. He looked at me, tilting his head back. I could see the thick veins running like wires beneath his pale skin. I wanted what flowed within them. I wanted Potter. I was in love with him, despite what he had done, and I hated myself for feeling like that. Taking a step closer, so our bodies brushed against each other's, I reached out with my right hand and placed it gently on the nape of his neck. His skin felt ice-cold. Potter closed his eyes as my lips brushed against his neck. I placed my left hand into his coat pocket and reached for what I knew he had hidden there. I curled my fingers around one of the glass bottles.

"You lie," I whispered in his ear, then pulled away.

Snapping his eyes open, Potter looked down at the glass tube of Lot-13 I held in my hand. "How did you know they were there?" he asked.

"The bulge in your coat pocket," I said, taking no satisfaction from discovering that he had lied to me again. "I would've had to be blind not to have *seen* that."

"It could have been anything," he said, with a sideways smile, knowing that he had been caught out again.

"I heard them clinking in your pocket," I explained.

"So you have super-duper hearing, as well as sight now?" Potter smirked. "Is that a wolf thing?"

"You bastard," I breathed, rolling my free hand into a fist and smashing it into the bridge of his nose. Potter's head rocked backwards as a fine spray of what looked like white dust seeped from between my clenched fingers.

Potter shook his head from side to side and looked at me. He said nothing.

"So you hate me now, is that it?" I snapped at him. "You hate me because you know I'm part Lycanthrope? We all know how much you hate the wolves."

"I don't hate you," Potter said, his eyes fixed on mine. "I love you, Kiera."

"You have a funny way of showing it," I said, unscrewing the cap on the glass tube. My fingers trembled as it came free in my hand. "You've lied to me."

"I didn't mean to," Potter said, his voice calm, just above a whisper.

I threw my head back and let the red stuff wash over my tongue. Its taste was bitter, a poor substitute for the real thing, but it would do. At once, those hunger pangs in my stomach eased. As I re-screwed the cap, I glanced at my hands and watched those tiny cracks fade again. For how long, I didn't know. I placed the empty tube into my pocket, and wiped the last of the Lot-13 from my lips with my fingers. I then licked them clean, not wanting to waste one drop.

"Better?" Potter asked.

"Not that you care," I snapped at him. The hunger inside of me had quickly been replaced with anger for Potter.

"I cared enough to come after you..." he started.

"Yeah, so you keep saying," I sneered. "You took your time, but now I know why. You were too busy getting it on with that teacher – the wolf."

"I thought she was you, Kiera," Potter started to explain. "She did that mind-fuck thing on me. She messed with my brains."

"That must have taken all of two seconds," I barked at him.

Ignoring my remark, Potter continued. "She was trying to frame me...Jack Seth was trying to set me up. His plan was for you to hate me...so you would choose him over me."

"I'm not going to choose anyone," I said coldly. "The only side I'm on is my own from now on."

"And that's just what he wanted," Potter said, coming across the empty room towards me. The floorboards creaked beneath his boots. "He wants to drive a wedge between us."

"You drove the wedge between us!" I hissed at him. "You lied to me about Murphy coming back. You lied about knowing my father was alive in this world..."

"I did it to protect you..." Potter cut in.

"And what about Sophie? Huh?" I said, folding my arms across my chest. "Sneaking off to see her was protecting me too?"

"In a way," Potter said thoughtfully. "She was the only person I could think of in this *pushed* world who might know what the fuck was going on."

"And where is she now?" I shot at him. "Keeping a bed nice and warm for you somewhere?"

"She's dead!" Potter snapped back, losing that calmness he had fought so long to hold on to. "Nothing happened between us."

"You expect me to believe that?" I said, remembering how the Elders had shown me a statue of Potter and Sophie together. "You're in love with her. You end up with her – not with me!" I screamed at him.

"What are you talking about?" Potter shouted, looking lost and bewildered.

"It doesn't matter," I breathed, turning away. How did I explain what I had seen, when I didn't truly understand it myself?

I heard the floorboards creak again as Potter came and stood behind me. He didn't dare come too close – leaving a foot or two between us. "Nothing happened between me and Sophie because I love you, Kiera," he said, his voice sounding softer again. "You've got to believe me."

"And Eloisa?" I pushed.

"I've explained that," Potter sighed out loud. "She tricked me..."

"Another wolf who messed with your brains," I sneered. Then turning to look at him, I added, "I was wrong about you. I don't think you hate wolves at all. It's all just been an act. You can't get enough of them."

"I hate them," Potter said, fixing his dead black eyes on mine. "I hate every last one of them."

"Then you hate me, too," I said, turning away.

Silence fell between us, as if both of us had run out of words to say. I smelt the scent of a freshly lit cigarette, then the sound of Potter crossing back towards the bedroom door. He paused.

"I do love you, Kiera Hudson, but I just don't know how to get you to believe me," he said. "But one thing I do know is that no one could hate you as much as you hate yourself."

Potter left me standing alone in the room. I watched Murphy through the window as he readied the police van for our journey to the Dead Waters.

Chapter Two

Potter

Why did she have to be so impossible? I roared inside, heading back down the stairs. I only lied about not having any bottles of the red stuff so I could have a kiss. Is that so fucking bad? But I knew it was more than just the lie about the red stuff. It was all of the shit I had managed to get myself into. Shit that Kiera didn't deserve. Did she really think I would hate her because she was part wolf? I couldn't give a monkey's toss if she was half chimpanzee – I loved her regardless. But what was the point? I might as well give up. I was only going to have my heart ripped out, stomped all over. That had happened once before. Sophie had taken out my heart and walked all over it. But that was going to feel like nothing compared to how hurt I would feel if I lost Kiera. Sophie would have merely tiptoed all over my heart, whereas losing Kiera would feel like it had been torn out and trampled over by a fucking army. That was gonna hurt real bad when it came. But what could I do to stop that fast-approaching army? I'd tried to tell her how things had happened. I'd tried to tell her how much I loved her. How come it had been easier talking to Kayla about my feelings for Kiera, than it was in person?

"What the fuck's wrong with you?" I heard Murphy suddenly bark. "You look suicidal."

I glanced up to find myself outside and in the cold. Murphy was standing by the police van.

"Nothing's wrong," I lied, flicking the cigarette end into the snow.

"Bollocks," Murphy grunted, brushing the last of the snow from the van's windscreen. "I heard you and Kiera

15

shouting at each other. It sounded like an episode of the freaking Jeremy Kyle show."

"Just keep your nose out of it," I told him. "It has nothing to do with you."

"Wrong," Murphy said, his back to me. "It has everything to do with me, I'm Kiera's uncle."

"So you'll be buying her Christmas presents next and taking her to the park to play on the fucking swings?" I snapped, taking another cigarette from the crumpled packet in my pocket.

"What's that s'posed to mean?" Murphy shot back, looking over his shoulder at me.

"Well, it's a bit late in the day for all this overprotective bullshit, don't you think?" I came back, cigarette dangling from the corner of my mouth. "We're only in this mess because of you."

"Are you taking drugs?" Murphy said, coming from around the side of the van in the snow. "You're in the crapper because you can't keep your dick in your pants. It's not me who has been waving it around like it's going out of fashion! To be honest, I've never understood how you've ever managed to get so much action."

"I'm not talking about my sex life," I growled. Then quickly added, "Besides, why shouldn't I have had lots of woman action? What's wrong with me?"

"What's wrong with you?" Murphy coughed, lighting his pipe. "Just take a good, hard look at yourself. You're untidy-looking. Your attitude stinks. You're violent. Your hatred for wolves borders on the psychotic, you're foul-mouthed, you chain smoke..."

"I'm not untidy-looking," I cut in, unable to believe he could think such a thing of me. "You take that back. That's a freaking lie if I ever heard one."

"Don't even get me started on the whole lying thing," Murphy snapped, taking the pipe from the corner of his mouth and pointing it at me.

"I don't lie," I shot at him.

"Yeah, you do," he grunted.

"When?" I demanded.

"Every time your lips move," he said.

"Yeah, very funny, you miserable old fart," I said. "You lied to Kiera, too. You've known for years the truth about her, but..."

"I was trying to protect her," Murphy interrupted.

"And so was I!" I snapped at him.

"You have a funny way of showing it!" Murphy barked.

"It wasn't me who got Kiera involved in this," I said, blowing smoke from my nostrils. "If you hadn't had arranged for her to come to the Ragged Cove, then none of this would have ever happened."

"Do you really believe that?" Murphy said, almost choking on a throat full of pipe smoke. "Kiera is special. She is unlike my daughters, who withered away, even though they were mixed with me – a Vampyrus – and a wolf. For some reason, Kiera survived – grew strong. Ravenwood, Hunt, and the Elders might not have known the true reason why, but all of them knew that there is something extraordinary about her. I arranged for Kiera to come to the Ragged Cove so I could keep an eye on her...to protect..."

"To protect you," I said in anger. "Once your brother had died, and with Kiera's adoptive mother gone missing in the Ragged Cove, you knew she was vulnerable on her own. You feared that the Elders might find out about your lies. You were shit-scared they would discover the truth about you and this wolf, Pen, about your brother and Kathy Seth..."

17

"And Kiera!" Murphy barked at me. "If they had discovered the truth, Kiera could have been in mortal danger. I needed to keep her close. That's the only reason I got into this. Besides, not even in my wildest fantasies did I ever think things would turn out this bad."

"How else did you think it would turn out, knowing the secrets you were keeping from everyone?" I came back at him.

"What do you mean, *everyone*? Who's everyone?" Murphy growled, sounding confused.

"You never told *me* the truth about what Kiera really is," I said.

"And why should I have done that?" Murphy frowned.

"Because you knew I'd fallen in love with her..." I started.

"So, knowing that Kiera was half-wolf would've made a difference, would it?" Murphy shouted.

I looked at him silently.

"Well, would it?" A voice said before I'd the chance to answer. I span around to find Kiera standing in the open cottage doorway. "Well?"

"No," I said. Knowing that one word sounded weak and insignificant, I quickly added, "If I'd known, I would have been able to protect you."

"I can take care of myself," she said, looking at both me and Murphy.

We both fell silent.

"Where did you last see Kayla and Sam?" she asked, diverting the conversation away from her.

"About five miles from here," Murphy said softly, placing the pipe back into the corner of his mouth.

"Over there," I added, pointing into the distance, which really wasn't of great help, but I wanted to say something – *anything.* Kiera had caught us off guard discussing her, and I wanted to move on from that as quickly as possible. I didn't want her to dwell on the fact that knowing she was a half-wolf would somehow change my feelings for her.

Looking at us, Kiera said, "If you've both quit bitching, I say we go and find our friends, don't you?"

Without saying another word, and pulling her coat tight, Kiera headed over to the van and climbed into the back. I watched her go, her black hair, which shone almost navy blue in the winter sun, billowing out behind her in the wind. Her face was pale, but way more than just beautiful, and I regretted the situation I now found myself in with her. I silently wished we could at last find some peace between us. I didn't want to fight anymore with Kiera. I just wanted to be with her. I wanted that day to come where I could take her on the date I'd always promised her. Were we ever going to catch a break? I wondered.

"Now look what you've gone and done," Murphy hissed under his breath at me.

"What?" I glared at him.

"You've gone and upset Kiera again," he said.

"Piss off, Sarge," I snapped back.

Scowling at me, Murphy grunted and hoisted himself up into the van. "You heard what Kiera said, numb-nuts, let's go and find Kayla and Sam."

I ignored his comment and clambered into the passenger seat. As Murphy started the van, the engine rumbling into life, I peered over my shoulder. Kiera sat alone in the back. She was hidden in shadow. If it hadn't have been for the glow of her bright hazel eyes, I would've never known she was there. I wanted to go and be with her, but I knew now wasn't the right time. I should give her some space. I faced front again, as Murphy rolled the police van slowly forward in the snow. The giant tyres crunched over the fresh white powder. We headed down the path, away from the cottage, the snow making it look like it had been showered with a million shards of twinkling glass.

"Take me to the exact spot where you last saw Kayla and Sam," Kiera said from the darkness behind us. "I want to know what I can *see*."

Chapter Three

Kiera

I sat in the back of the police van as it made its way through the snow and ice. Murphy struggled at times to keep the vehicle on the road. It had stopped snowing hours ago, but the twisty tracks and roads which spiralled away from my father's house where covered in drifts of powdery snow and slush. Not one of us spoke as we made our way across the bleak-looking country towards the place where Murphy and Potter had last seen our friends. What had happened to them? I wondered. Although everything I had learnt in the last twenty-four hours kept fogging my mind, I tried to force it away. What was the point on dwelling on it now? I couldn't let my own pain and hurt blind me from finding Sam and Kayla. Sam, I didn't know well, but he had proved himself useful in a fight, and if nothing more, I could tell Kayla was fond of him. She had already lost her brother, Isidor, and I didn't want her to suffer any more loss if I could help it.

I loved Kayla like a sister and I wasn't going to give up on her. With what little Murphy and Potter had told me about Kayla and Sam's disappearance, I suspected something bad had happened to them. Kayla wouldn't have just gone, leaving her friends behind. As I sat in the back of the van and watched the white-coated world drift slowly past, I knew I could have pressed both Murphy and Potter for more information, but I didn't want to. Not because I was angry with them; I could push my feelings aside to keep focused on the mission before me. I didn't ask them for any more information because I didn't want to be tainted by it. I would go to the scene of Kayla and Sam's disappearance with an open mind. I didn't need any preconceived ideas to cloud my judgement. I wanted to visit the scene fresh and *see* it for the first time.

So closing my eyes, I settled back in my seat. Resting my hands on my knees, I took a deep breath and tried to clear my mind. But however much I tried to focus on nothing, Jack Seth appeared before me. I couldn't help but see him as a small boy. I couldn't help but feel his pain. Where was he now? I wondered. He was out there, somewhere in the snow. But doing what, exactly? What did he have planned? Jack always had a plan. Should I have set him free? Should I have let Potter and Murphy kill him? They would have done it. No, I couldn't have done that. Not just because Jack was my half-brother; there was more to it than that. Jack was a bad man – of that, there was no doubt. If I had handed him over to Murphy and Potter to deal with, he wouldn't have received a fair hearing. Didn't everyone deserve that at least? To have given him up, I might as well have killed him myself. I didn't want Jack dead – there was good in him, I was sure of it. I felt it. I saw it in his eyes and heard it in his voice as he had told me his story. That little boy was still inside of him somewhere. And he knew more than any of us did about this world. He said he knew the photographer. Jack had talked about layers – different levels – worlds that had been *pushed*. He had told me to find the wolf named Lilly Blu – who had once been known by another name. She had been the wolf Murphy had risked so much for. Penelope Flack had been the woman he had loved. She was a part of this. Jack had hinted that she might know how to *push* this world back. Did Murphy know that she was here in this world? No, I didn't think so. Should I tell him? Didn't he have a right to know? If I didn't tell him, then I was keeping a secret like the secret he had kept from me. I would tell him, but not now. When we were alone next. How would he feel knowing that the woman he loved – the mother of his two daughters,

Meren and Nessa, was alive in this world – and that she possibly knew the identity of the photographer, and how we might *push* the world back?

"This is the place," Murphy suddenly said. I snapped open my eyes and stared through the window. We had stopped alongside a snow-covered field. In the distance there was a barn. I slid open the side door of the van and climbed out. It was cold and bleak. The hills rolled away into the distance, so white, they almost seemed to blend into the snow-laden sky. I crossed in front of the van and headed towards a small stone slate wall, which ran the length of the narrow road.

"We last saw Kayla and Sam in this field," Murphy said, pointing into the distance.

"Any tracks will be covered by now," Potter said, joining us at the wall.

"Not necessarily," I said, clambering over the wall and into the field. I landed in the snow. Potter and Murphy climbed over the wall behind me. I turned to look at them. Raising my hand, I said, "Keep back, we don't want any tracks trampled over."

I caught Potter shoot a sideways glance at Murphy. That look reminded me of being back in the Ragged Cove. It reminded me of how Potter had called me 'Miss Marple.' Did he still think the same, or was that me just being paranoid? I pushed the memory from my mind and surveyed the scene before me.

"Now what do I *see*?" I whispered, slowly setting off across the field.

Chapter Four

Potter

Maybe the signs that Kiera had always been part wolf had always been there, but I'd been too dumb to notice. As Kiera dropped low and worked her way across the field, she looked something close to a giant bloodhound wrapped in a long, dark coat. She paused, looked closely at the ground, then moved on again, weaving her way across the field. Kiera would stop suddenly and run the tips of her fingers over the snow. She would take some, hold it up to the light, then let if fall from between her fingers. Fuck knows what Kiera was able to see. To me it just looked like a bunch of white stuff.

Sometimes she appeared methodical in her examination, other times more frenzied, as she darted forward, stopped for a moment, as if getting her bearings, spinning around in a spray of snow, then racing forward again. I watched as several times, she dropped completely onto her front. Then, as if she were burying her face in the snow, she would make an examination of the ground and whatever else it was she could see.

Murphy and I watched from the wall, occasionally sharing a quick glance at each other, then back at Kiera. With a look of pride on his face, Murphy whispered, "Look at her go. You can tell she's a chip off the old block."

"What's that s'posed to mean?" I frowned.

"She's a natural copper – a natural investigator, just like me," Murphy said, puffing out his chest and sucking on his pipe.

"You couldn't solve a crime even if you stumbled across a killer standing over a headless copse with an axe in his hand

shouting, 'I'm glad I chopped the arsehole's freaking head off!'"
I groaned. "You're nothing like Kiera."

"She takes after me, alright," Murphy said thoughtfully
as he watched Kiera at work. "We're definitely related."

"And you say I'm the one who is taking fucking drugs," I
sighed, stepping away from the wall and Murphy. He was
starting to piss me off with this newfound admiration and
concern for Kiera. It was like now that the truth about her
being his niece was out, he had to take credit for every little
thing she did.

I continued to watch Kiera zigzag across the field as she
made her way towards a line of trees in the distance. Reaching
them, she stopped, hunkered down again briefly, then stood
up. Turning to face us, she beckoned us towards her with a
wave of her hand.

"Looks like she's found something," I said over my
shoulder, but Murphy was already passing by me.

"Just like I said she would," Murphy grunted, heading
out across the field towards Kiera.

"*Just like I said she would,*" I mimicked under my breath,
following Murphy across the field.

With plumes of breath escaping my mouth and
disappearing up into the fresh morning air, I reached the line of
trees with Murphy.

"What have you found, Kiera?" he asked.

Nodding back in the direction that we had come, Kiera
said, "Okay, so over there is where you, Kayla, and Sam fought
with wolves. There were seven of them..."

"Seven different tracks," Murphy cut in knowingly.

"Right," Kiera said. "Potter was being held face down
and that's where he took a beating..."

"Blood splatters," Murphy cut in again, glancing at me
with a smug smile.

"Right," Kiera said. "The fight was fierce, but over quickly. One of the wolves was decapitated, I'm guessing by you, Murphy, as Potter was face down in the snow, and Kayla and Sam were fighting with wolves just over there."

"Yes it was me," Murphy said, puffing his chest out in pride.

"Okay, so while you were distracted by the fight, another person appeared. This one didn't join the fight. Whoever it was, was watching from the edge of this treeline."

"How can you be so sure?" I asked.

"See the footprints?" Kiera said, pointing at the ground beneath a nearby tree.

I looked and could see them. The snow wasn't as deep beneath the trees, but they hadn't been filled in either by more falling snow – so they were clearer than any other tracks she had managed to find.

"Kayla and Sam ran across the field towards her," Kiera started.

"Her?" I asked. "How can you be so sure it was a female?"

"She was wearing boots with a small heel," Kiera explained, dropping to her knees and pointing to the footprints in the snow.

"So how do you know Kayla and Sam ran towards her?" I asked. It wasn't that I didn't believe her, but I was tired of Murphy jumping in with his explanations.

"By the distance between each footprint," Murphy cut in anyway. "If someone is running, the gap between each footprint will be larger than if they were walking."

"Correct!" Kiera said. "But don't forget that the toe of the shoe will be more pronounced, again suggesting running instead of merely walking."

"So what happened when they reached this point?" I asked.

"They stood and talked to whoever she was," Kiera said. "You can see by the spread of prints they stood here for a little while before heading off through the trees with the female."

"Where did they go?" I tried to follow the prints, but the snow just looked like a trampled mess.

"Let's find out," Kiera said, setting off between the trees.

We followed behind as she sometimes raced ahead, then slowed to an almost standstill. She would inspect the ground again, then set off. We followed at a distance, both of us mindful not to get in her way or destroy any evidence. Then, up ahead, Kiera came to a sudden halt.

"What's wrong?" I asked, joining her beneath a large oak tree.

"The tracks just suddenly stop," Kiera said with a frown, looking down at the ground. "It's like the three of them just vanished."

"Vanished?" Murphy grunted.

"Perhaps this other person they met was a Vampyrus and they flew away?" I suggested, believing it to be a reasonable possibility.

"Sam's a wolf and can't fly," Murphy said.

"Maybe Kayla carried him?" I said, not wanting my theory to be proved wrong – not just seconds after formulating it.

"And perhaps an army of pixies appeared and sprayed them all with magic disappearing dust?" Murphy scowled at me.

"No one flew away," Kiera cut in, as if trying to diffuse the growing tension between me and Murphy.

"How can you tell?" I asked her.

Looking up, Kiera said, 'See how the branches of the trees are so close together? If they had flown away from here, they would have disturbed the branches and the snow would have fallen away. But as you can see, they are still covered in a thick layer of snow."

"So what do you think happened to them?" Murphy asked.

"I don't know," Kiera whispered thoughtfully. "I just don't know."

"Well, standing out here isn't going to help us find them," Murphy said, turning away. "Good job, Kiera, but if the tracks have run cold, then we need to start looking someplace else."

"Where?" I asked, watching him walk away.

"Kayla and Sam knew we were heading for the Fountain of Souls and the Dead Waters," Murphy said, glancing back at us. "Perhaps they will head there."

"But how can they have just vanished, into thin air?" I frowned. "And who is this female they were talking to? Kayla wouldn't have just walked away and left me and Murphy to get the shit kicked out of us. How do we know Teen Wolf hasn't taken her, we don't even know if we can trust him? You know what happens to a human who has been badly matched to a wolf, they turn in to those freaky fucking berserkers! Sam might have become one of them and eaten Kayla."

"Have you been sniffing fucking glue?" Murphy rounded on me. "Jesus Christ, you make Sam sound like the big bad wolf out of little-red-freaking-riding-hood!"

I looked at Kiera, and without saying a word, she set off after Murphy. I followed at a distance as we made our way out of the small woods and back across the field. I looked back and could see the barn where I had been tricked into believing that teacher had been Kiera. I remembered how I had killed the wolf-boy, Dorsey, and how that hooded photographer had appeared and taken a photo of him dead in my arms. I looked away, and it was then I saw several of those creepy statues standing in a row on the other side of the field. I opened my mouth to call out after Kiera and Murphy. But what was the point? Neither of them seemed to be interested in anything I had to say. I closed my mouth, turned away from the statues, and caught up with Kiera and Murphy.

As I walked silently alongside them, Murphy looked sideways at Kiera, and trying to sound knowledgeable, he said, "What I can't figure out is how you knew I decapitated one of those skinwalkers. Was it blood splatter patterns again?"

"No," Kiera said, looking straight ahead.

"What then?" Murphy frowned.

"You left its freaking head behind," Kiera said, striding ahead, back towards the van.

Murphy stopped in his tracks and watched her go, his mouth open wide.

I couldn't help but secretly smile to myself.

Chapter Five

Kiera

I scrambled over the wall and dropped down onto the other side. I couldn't explain where Kayla and Sam had suddenly disappeared to, and that troubled me. It frustrated me. What wasn't I *seeing*? As far as I could tell, there was nothing left to see once those tracks had come to a sudden halt. It really was like Kayla, Sam, and this other female had just vanished into thin air. Had this something to do with the layers that Jack had mentioned?

Both Potter and Murphy leapt over the wall behind me, their feet thudding onto the hard-packed snow. I glanced back at them; both were dressed in black police-issue coats. They both looked worn and beat up. Potter's bruises had almost faded away as his body quickly healed from the beating he had taken out in the field. Had he received such punishment coming to recue me? The thought made me feel sorry for him. But I didn't want to feel like that. Not yet – I was still too hurt, angry, and confused.

Potter caught me looking at him, and raising an eyebrow, he said, "What?"

"Nothing," I whispered, turning away and sliding open the van door.

Potter brushed past me as I climbed inside, his hand deliberately coming to rest against my thigh. As he went, he leaned in close to me and whispered, "You may hate me, sweet-cheeks, but you just can't stop looking at me."

"Dream on," I muttered under my breath, yanking the van door closed in his face. I caught sight of Potter smirking to himself as he climbed into the seat next to Murphy. I so badly wanted to wipe that smile from his arrogant looking face. I clenched my fists and sat on them.

"Looks like we've got company," Murphy suddenly said from the front of the van.

I glanced up to see a car heading down the narrow lane towards us. Although it was just black in colour, we knew it was an unmarked police car, because of the removable blue light attached to the roof. "Real cops or Skin-walkers?" I breathed.

"Either way, we're fucked," Potter said. "It isn't going to take them too long to figure out we're the ones who ripped up their friends back here yesterday. I knew it was a bad idea coming back to this field."

"You never said," I reminded him.

"Would you have listened?" Potter remarked, glancing over his shoulder at me.

"Let me do the talking," Murphy said, swinging open the van door once more and climbing out.

Leaning forward in my seat, I watched Murphy stand in front of the van. The other police vehicle crawled slowly down the track, its thick tyres throwing up snow and slush. I peered ahead and could see four cops wedged into the unmarked patrol car.

"There's four of them," I told Potter.

Without saying anything back, Potter pushed open the van door and climbed out.

"Where are you going?" I hissed. "Murphy said to leave it up to him."

Potter slammed the door shut and joined Murphy in front of the van. *Here we go again,* I thought to myself, sliding open the van door and jumping out. I joined Murphy and Potter as the car came to a juddering halt in the snow. Murphy and Potter gave each other one quick, knowing look. It was like

31

they had some kind of telepathic link. But despite their constant bickering and sniping at each other, they were a team – a partnership. Both were able to anticipate the other's next move and both had each other's back. It seemed that no father and son or any two brothers had the loyalty these two men showed one another when they were in trouble. Their friendship was unbreakable.

The driver's door to the patrol car slowly creaked open. A giant of a man climbed out of the vehicle. His police cap was pressed flat on the top of his huge, round head, the beak pulled down too far; the rim almost touched the tip of his long nose. He was dressed all in black, his police uniform immaculate – something Murphy would have been proud of. From the passenger's seat climbed another cop. This one was smaller than the first, but carried in his hand a long, black rod which hissed and spat tiny blue sparks. The back doors opened on either side of the vehicle like a set of wings. The last two cops climbed out, and I could see that one of them was female. The four cops came forward.

Standing before us, the huge cop looked bigger, like some kind of freaky giant. The other swung the Taser in his fist like a club. The last two hung back.

"Who are you?" the giant cop asked, his dark eyes peering out at us from beneath the beak of his cap.

"We're cops," Potter said.

Now I don't know if Potter was being a wise arse, but all the same, it seemed like a stupid thing to say.

"I can see that," the cop growled, his voice sounding deep and throaty.

I saw the two silver pips on each of his shoulders. He was an Inspector, and he outranked Murphy.

"You'll have to forgive Constable Gabriella," Murphy cut in. "He is still young in service. He obviously didn't understand your question."

"How many ways have I got to tell you, Sarge – its Gabriel! Gabriella is a freaking girl's name!" Potter glared at Murphy.

The Inspector looked at both Murphy and Potter in disbelief as they stood and argued. "Listen here, you couple of morons, I couldn't give a crap what your name is. You need to get your act together and smarten up. Just look at yourselves. You're a complete mess."

"See, Gabriella, I told you you're untidy and need to smarten yourself up," Murphy grunted. "But oh no, you wouldn't listen to me. And now the Inspector has seen you looking like a sack of shit, and we're both in trouble."

"I don't look like a sack of shit!" Potter snapped back at Murphy, taking a cigarette from his coat pocket and lighting it. "I wear my uniform with pride. Anyway, you've got no room to talk – you're wearing carpet slippers, for fuck's sake!"

"Is this some sort of a joke?" the Inspector roared. "I don't believe what I'm hearing and seeing. How dare you stand there and smoke..."

"Shit! I'm sorry, guvnor," Potter said, taking another cigarette from his coat pocket and offering it to the Inspector. "How rude of me – I should have offered you one, too."

"If you don't fancy a cigarette, I've got a pipe you can have a suck on," Murphy cut in, fishing his pipe from his coat pocket.

The Inspector looked at both Murphy and Potter as if dumbstruck. Then, as if noticing me for the first time, he said, "And who are you, the sidekick?" Unlike my friends, I wasn't dressed in police uniform.

Before I'd had a chance to say anything, Potter cut in and said, "This is our prisoner. We've arrested her."

"For what?" the Inspector scowled, and just for a moment, I saw a spark of yellow glint in his dull eyes. Potter had been right. We were fucked.

"For killing all those cops out here yesterday," Murphy said, now puffing thoughtfully on his pipe.

The Inspector eyed me up and down, then looked back at Murphy. "You seriously expect me to believe that this young girl was responsible for killing all those police officers yesterday?"

"Yep," Murphy said, blowing smoke casually from between his lips.

From the corner of my eye, I saw the two cops at the back reach for their long Taser sticks.

"I know she doesn't look like much, but you should see her in action. Believe me she can be a real *tiger* when she wants to be," Potter smiled at the Inspector. Then winking at me, Potter added, "Isn't that right?"

"Sure is," I said, swinging my arm at speed towards the Inspector. Without even having to think about it, my razor-sharp claws sprang from my fingers and buried themselves in the Inspector's throat. A jet of hot, black blood shot back at me, splashing my face. The Inspector threw his hands to his throat. They gripped my wrist, trying to pull my claws from his jugular. His blood pumped over my fist and down my arm in hot, sticky waves. He made a gargling sound in the back of his throat as he tried to scream. Blood sprayed from his open mouth and coated Potter.

"Now my uniform *is* a mess," he groaned, tearing the coat from his back as he sprang into the air. In a flutter of black shadows, his wings were free. He clasped the head of the nearest cop in his claws. With one sudden and blindingly quick

34

twist, he tore the cop's head clean off. The head came away from the neck so clean and fast, that the body stood momentarily in the snow, until it toppled over.

The Inspector stopped struggling and fell still. I slid my claws from the jagged hole they had made in his throat. He collapsed backwards into the snow, where the blood pumping from his throat turned the road crimson. I ran the back of my hand down the side of my face, wiping away the splashes of blood that were there. With my stomach leaping at the sight and smell of the blood, and knowing that the Lot-13 was close to running out, I closed my eyes and licked my fingers clean. The Inspector's blood felt hot and tasted sweet in my mouth. I swallowed hard and felt the blood warm the back of my throat. It felt more than good, but I didn't want to come to enjoy that sensation.

I opened my eyes to see the last two remaining cops pulling their uniforms free as their bodies bristled with fur. I stared at the female officer in fascination and with morbid curiosity, as her body began to twist and stretch out of shape as she took the form of a wolf. Her fur was white and sleek, covering her long, slender body from head to toe. An elegant-looking tail snaked from her hind quarters as she leapt into the air, her jaws foaming. *Was there something like that hiding deep inside of me?* I feared, ripping my coat free. With my wings springing from my back, I lunged at her. We met mid-air, clattering onto one another. She howled, her giant jaws spraying foam just inches from my face. The little black claws at the tips of my wings grabbed for her as we spun around and around in the air. Her fur felt like silk as I raked my claws along the length of her back. She barked and yelped in pain as we fell through the sky. As the ground raced up towards us, I saw Murphy removing his uniform and folding it into a neat pile on the driver's seat of the police van. He didn't seem to be in any hurry.

We thudded into the snow. With my huge black wings arrowed out behind me, I sat astride the wolf as it kicked wildly out with its back legs, trying to scratch at my face with is giant front paws. The wolf's bright yellow eyes rolled in their wet sockets. The thought that somewhere deep inside of me was a wolf just like this one terrified me. With fear and dread consuming me, I clawed and ripped frantically at the fighting wolf. My claws sliced and slashed open giant wounds. Slick-looking entrails and tufts of blood-soaked fur shot up into the air as I tore the wolf to pieces. Somewhere inside of me, a voice was urging me on. It was as if by killing this wolf, I was killing the one I feared hiding deep within me.

Suddenly, I felt a firm hand grip my shoulder. "That's enough," I heard a voice say.

Covered in blood, flesh, and fur, I opened my eyes. Murphy was leaning over me and looking into my face. "The wolf is dead, Kiera. The wolf is *dead*."

Slowly, I stopped clawing and tearing. Gasping for air, I clambered off what was left of the wolf. Murphy helped me to my feet. I stood in the scarlet snow, panting and sighing, my face, arms and wings dripping with blood.

"What have I done?" I panted, looking at Murphy.

"What needed to be done, if any of us were to survive," he said flatly.

"I tore it to shreds," I said, blood dripping from my claws and spattering the snow at my feet.

"And it wouldn't have thought twice about doing the same to you," Potter said, suddenly appearing beside me.

His long, black tattered wings hung from his back, the tips of them trailing in the snow. He was naked to the waist, and his well-defined body was splashed with blood, as were his claws and forearms. I had to fight the sudden urge to be held by him, to be pressed against him. To feel that warm, sticky blood and his body moving against mine. I looked away.

"I killed the last of them, Sarge," Potter breathed deeply.

"Not the last of them," Murphy grunted. "Just the start of them. There are plenty more where they came from."

I looked at Murphy.

"Let's clean this mess up and get on our way," Murphy added, heading back towards the road.

Chapter Six

Kiera

Together we carried the remains of the wolves down the lane and hid them beneath the snow-covered bracken and thistles at the edge of a ditch.

"What we can't find, the foxes will eat," Murphy said.

I felt soiled and dirty somehow, and although earlier I had enjoyed the taste of the Inspector's blood. I now just wanted to be rid of it. I wanted to shower and scrub the blood of those wolves from my body. I was desperate to wear some clean clothes. We trudged back up the road, towards the police van and the unmarked patrol car. It was then I spied the female officer's uniform scattered along the lane wear she had pulled it free during her transformation into a wolf. Bending down, I gathered up the clothes. I went to the back of the van, climbed inside, and closed the door.

Alone, I began to undress. The passenger side door suddenly flew open, and Potter was looking in at me. I crossed my arms over my breasts.

"Do you mind?" I snapped at him.

"What are you doing?" Potter asked, staring at me.

"Getting out of these blood-soaked clothes, what does it look like?" I hissed.

"Okay, but hurry up. The Sarge wants to get going," Potter shut the door, leaving me alone again.

I screwed my dirty, torn clothes into a ball and stuffed them under the nearest seat. Then, almost bent double in the confined space at the back of the van, I put on the female officer's uniform. As I buttoned up the shirt, I couldn't remember the last time I had worn a police uniform. It must have been back in the Ragged Cove, I thought. That seemed like a whole lifetime ago now. Once dressed, I clambered from the van and back out into the cold. Potter was leaning against the van, smoking a cigarette. He looked me up and down. I closed the van door and headed towards the unmarked car where Murphy was removing the blue emergency light from the roof.

"Hey, tiger," Potter said gripping hold of my arm and spinning me around to face him.

"What?" I said, looking into his dark eyes.

"Seeing you dressed like this again reminds me of why I fell in love with you," he smiled at me.

"How come?" I asked.

Leaning in close, Potter whispered in my ear, "I'd forgotten how damn good your sweet cheeks looked in uniform."

I eased myself away from him, sliding my arm from his grip. "We should get going," I said. "Murphy's right, more of those Skin-walkers could come back at any time." Turning my back and leaving him alone by the van, I made my way down the narrow country lane towards Murphy.

"Get in," Murphy said, as I reached the vehicle.

"What about the van?" I asked.

"We're gonna stand out in that," he said. "If we're going to reach the Dead Waters alive, we need to keep our heads down. We can't afford to draw any more unwanted attention to ourselves. Riding around in a big white van with luminous yellow and blue squares all over it ain't my idea of being inconspicuous."

"So, where to now?" I said, climbing into the passenger seat. I knew Potter always liked to sit up front, and I smiled inwardly as I took my seat next to Murphy.

"We find somewhere to clean up and get some rest," Murphy said. Then, without warning he blasted the horn three times. The sound was deafening and echoed back off the fields and rolling hills. Leaning out of the window, he hollered at Potter, "Stop standing there with your thumb up your arse! We need to be out of here already."

"I thought we weren't meant to be drawing any attention to ourselves?" I said, the sound of the horn still ringing in my ears.

Murphy grunted and started the engine.

Potter mooched down the road, the tails of his long, black coat flapping around his legs, like his wings so often did. He looked at me sitting up front, scowled like a schoolboy, and climbed into the back, slamming the door behind him.

"Everything okay?" I asked, trying to hide a smile.

"Just perfect," he sniped, shutting his eyes and leaning back in his seat.

Taking great care in the snow, Murphy steered the car around the abandoned police van, and in silence, we headed down the desolate road and towards the hills in the distance.

We drove for what seemed like hours across the bleakest land I had ever seen. The sky had turned from white to a dirty, washed-out grey, and I suspected that another storm was on its way. Conversation was non-existent between the three of us, and the atmosphere inside the car was as cold as the wind, which howled across the fields on either side of the roads we travelled. Every so often we would pass a derelict-looking outhouse, farmhouse, cottage, or barn. Murphy would slow and look at the building as it sailed past. I knew he was searching for some suitable place for us to stay for the night. The only places that looked semi inhabitable had smoke coiling up from the chimneys, telling us that they were already occupied by their rightful owners.

As the sky grew darker still, and the fresh flakes of snow began to swirl down from the sky, Murphy stopped the vehicle by a narrow lane, which wound away into the darkness to our right. Barely visible behind a clump of wild ivy, there was a sign sticking up out of the ditch which ran alongside the road. In red letters, the word 'Campsite' had been written. Without saying a word, Murphy turned into the narrow lane and headed up the hill.

"You've got to be kidding me," Potter suddenly spoke up from the back of the car.

"Got a better suggestion?" Murphy said.

"I don't want to piss all over your plan, Sarge, but this ain't the weather for camping," Potter groaned. "We haven't even got a tent."

"They'll have an empty caravan or two," Murphy said, his eyes fixed on the narrow lane ahead.

"What if they are all booked up?" Potter shot back.

"In this weather?" Murphy snapped. "Give me a break."

"Yeah, you're right," Potter said. "We're the only fucking Muppets dumb enough to take a camping holiday in sub-zero temperatures."

"Quit complaining," Murphy said, as we passed through an open gate. "It might be quite nice."

"I wouldn't describe freezing my freaking nuts off as being *nice*," Potter moaned. "Or perhaps you're planning on us all sitting around a campfire while you sing songs and pass around the marshmallows?"

"One more wisecrack from you, Potter, and I'm gonna smash you in the mouth," Murphy barked, pulling the vehicle to a halt outside a small cottage. Then, glancing at me, he added, "Zip that coat up and hide your uniform. We don't want anyone here knowing we're coppers. I don't think they're trusted in this world."

I zipped up my coat, and climbed from the car.

"What about me?" Potter asked.

"Stay here," Murphy ordered him.

"Why?" Potter said, looking hurt and left out.

"Because, I'm not planning on tearing the campsite owner a new arsehole, that's why," Murphy said, climbing from the car.

"What's that s'posed to mean?" Potter snapped.

"It means I want to find us a place to sleep for the night without all hell breaking loose," Murphy barked before slamming the car door in Potter's face.

Chapter Seven

Potter

Miserable old fart, I thought to myself as Murphy walked away from the car with Kiera. The old guy was getting crankier by the day. But Murphy was the least of my problems, we had always bitched at one another. It was my relationship with Kiera I was most worried about. How would I ever convince her it was just her I wanted – the person I loved most? I had fucked up a lot in my life, but this was the mother of all fuck-ups. If you could win the gold at the Olympics for the biggest screw-up, I'd be up there on the podium, clutching the gold, silver, and bronze medals.

How would I ever get her to listen to me? If only Kayla were here. She might be able to convince Kiera for me. But *I* had to tell Kiera; that was the whole point, wasn't it? How? I'd tried telling her, hadn't I? I even told her how hot she looked in the police uniform. All women want to hear that kinda shit, didn't they? I must be missing something – but what? Fuck if I knew what it was, I thought, scratching my head.

I took a cigarette from the crinkled packet in my pocket. There was only one left. Bollocks! I peered through the window and out into the night. There wasn't going to be a shop for freaking miles. Then, through the darkness and slow falling snow, I saw what looked like a small kiosk, the kind of place visitors to the campsite could buy maps of the local area, throwaway raincoats, and that sorta shit. Pushing open the car door, I climbed out. I looked back over my shoulder to see Kiera and Murphy talking to a thickset-looking guy standing in the open doorway of the cottage.

"Sorry, but we're closed for the winter," I heard the guy at the door say. "You're out of season by about three months."

"We only want to stay a night," Murphy said, fishing a roll of bank notes from his pocket.

I didn't doubt for a minute that Murphy would convince the campsite owner to let us use one of his caravans for the night. Murphy had his own unique way of convincing people to give him what he ultimately wanted. I looked away and headed through the wind and the snow to the small kiosk. It was locked up and the lights were out. Just like the guy said, we were out of season. Leaning against the wall of the kiosk was a Coke dispenser, and next to that was a cigarette machine.

"A tenner for a pack of smokes!" I breathed, reading the price printed on the front of the machine. "You've got to be kidding me." I knew I didn't have any money on me, and I wasn't going to go begging from Murphy.

I peered around the side of the kiosk and could see the others still talking outside the cottage. Turning back to the machine and extending my claws, I punched a hole in the front and grabbed for a pack of the cigarettes. Before I'd even had a chance to snatch a packet, a hideous alarm started to screech. It was ear-splitting.

"What's going on?" I heard the campsite owner boom.

I glanced around the edge of the kiosk again to see the guy step away from Murphy and Kiera and come rushing over to the kiosk.

"Shut the fuck-up!" I hissed at the machine, pounding the top of it with my fist. The alarm continued to scream its high-pitched wail into the night.

Knowing that I would never be able to silence the damn thing before the owner got to me, I reached inside and grabbed as many packs of smokes I could hold and began to stuff them into my coat pockets.

"What's going on here?" a voice suddenly boomed from behind me.

"Your freaking machine's throwing a fit, that's what's going on," I snapped. "It swallowed up my money quick enough and then wouldn't pay out."

"The front of it is smashed!" the man hollered, looking down at the machine.

"Probably the reason it's broken," I said, looking at him. "Kids these days! I don't know – bloody vandals the lot of them. Prison – that's what they need."

"What kids?" the man asked, reaching behind the machine and switching off the alarm.

"The kids who vandalised your machine," I told him. "Christ knows how kids are being raised these days. They were probably stealing the smokes for their parents..."

"Who are you?" the campsite owner suddenly cut in.

"He's with us," Murphy said, suddenly appearing around the side of the kiosk. Then, glaring at me, Murphy quickly added, "I thought I told you to wait in the car?"

"I'm not a freaking pet dog," I shot back.

"What's going on here?" the man cut in again, looking ever more confused with each passing moment.

"You'll have to forgive my nephew," Murphy said, looking back at the man. "He is a little bit simple – you know, has learning difficulties."

"Retarded, you mean?" the man asked, eyeing me, now with some pity in his eyes.

"I'm not a freaking re..." I started.

"And I'm his social worker," Kiera cut over me, taking me gently by the arm. Then, looking at me, she smiled sweetly and added, "Come on back to the car, Gabriel. You'll be safe and warm there. Let Uncle Murphy pay for the damage you've caused."

"This is un-fucking-believable...!" I started.

"Shhh now," Kiera hushed gently, easing me away by the arm. "Don't get yourself upset, Gabriel. We'll find some other place to stay tonight. Then tomorrow you'll be safe and sound back in your secure unit."

As Kiera led me around the side of the kiosk and back towards the car, I heard the campsite owner speak to Murphy and say, "Jeez, I didn't realise you had...a..."

"It's okay," Murphy cut in. "It's been a long drive and my poor nephew has become rather upset and confused."

"Look, I've got a couple of spare caravans you can use for the night. They're not much, they haven't been cleaned since last summer, but they're warm, and I'll switch on the hot water at the pump so you can all freshen up," the owner said, sounding apologetic.

"Please don't put yourself to any bother on our account," Murphy started.

"No bother at all," I heard the owner say. It looks like you've got enough to deal with. And besides, I wouldn't be able to rest knowing that I had turned you and your troubled nephew away."

"Troubled!" I hissed at Kiera, yanking my arm free. "I ain't troubled."

"Just be quiet," Kiera hissed at me. "You want somewhere warm to sleep tonight, don't you?"

"I'd rather sleep standing up in the freaking snow!" I spat.

"That can be arranged!" Kiera shot back.

"You're enjoying this, aren't you?" I whispered at her, as Murphy and the man headed back towards the cottage.

"Enjoying what?" she said, from the corner of her mouth.

"Watching me being humiliated like this," I said back. "You're not my freaking social worker!"

"So what am I?" Kiera snapped, looking at me. "What exactly do I mean to you?"

Everything, I wanted to say, but before I'd had a chance, Murphy was jangling two sets of keys in my face.

"Cheer up, Gabriel – we've got ourselves a place to sleep tonight."

"Awesome," I growled, watching Murphy and Kiera turn and head towards a row of desolate-looking caravans in the distance.

Chapter Eight

Potter

We reached a row of static caravans. They stretched away to the right and left, into the darkness. Murphy held the keys up and checked the door numbers, which were printed on little plastic tags.

"Twenty-four and twenty-five," he muttered to himself.

"Over here," Kiera said, heading towards two caravans that stood apart from the rest. These were bigger than the others and looked more like mobile homes. This must be where the more discerning camper stayed, I thought to myself as I followed her.

"You take twenty-five," Murphy said, handing Kiera the key to the mobile home.

Kiera took it, heading up a short set of concrete steps which led to the door. She opened it, switched on the light, then stepped inside.

"See you later, alligator," I said.

Kiera closed the door without saying anything. Perhaps she hadn't heard me, I thought.

"See you later, alligator?" Murphy grunted. "What's that s'posed to mean?"

"Forget it," I said, heading up the short set of steps to our mobile home.

Murphy followed, slipped the key into the lock, and pushed open the door. He flicked on the light, closing the door behind us. The mobile home was long and narrow. There was a sofa running down the length of the far wall, and I guessed it opened out to form a bed. There was a small T.V. set mounted on the wall with an iron bracket. On the other side of the room was a kitchenette with a cooker and fridge. To the right of Murphy, were two narrow doors set into a dividing wall. Murphy pushed one of them open.

"That's the crapper," he said. He peered behind the second door and added, "The bedroom."

"I'll take the sofa," I said crossing the room and flopping down onto it. The cushions were soft and spongy. I lay back, placed my fingers behind my head, and crossed my feet at the ankles.

"What's got into you?" Murphy mumbled. "You're about as much fun as the plague."

"You told that guy I had issues," I scowled.

"You do," Murphy said, turning on the hot tap over the sink. A stream of steaming water tumbled out. "The hot water's on so at least we can shower."

"You think it's all just a big laugh, don't you?" I said, looking at Murphy.

"What's that?" he said, turning off the tap and taking his pipe from his pocket.

"Me and Kiera," I told him. "It's not funny."

Sighing, Murphy sat at the end of the sofa and looked at me. "Okay, so I've been taking the piss a bit..." he started.

"A bit!" I scoffed. "You've been rubbing my nose in it all day. I'm just looking for a bit of advice here."

"I'm not your father," he said, holding a match over the bowl of his pipe.

"But I thought you were my friend," I said.

Blowing thick jets of blue smoke through his nostrils, Murphy looked at me and said, "Only you can sort this thing out with Kiera. No one can do it for you."

"I've tried," I told him.

"How?" Murphy said, his pipe drooping from the corner of his mouth. "Telling Kiera her butt looks nice in police uniform ain't going to get you anywhere. She isn't some old tart you're trying to get your leg over with. I thought she meant more to you than that."

"She does," I said, swinging my legs over the side of the sofa and sitting up.

"Then tell her," Murphy sighed with despair.

"I don't know how, that's my problem," I said, dropping my head. "I've never been very good with words."

"Who's talking about words," Murphy said. "You need to show her, Potter."

"What you mean? I should go over there and..." I started.

"No, for crying out loud, "Murphy interrupted. "Stop thinking with your goddamn dick for once!"

"How then?" I said, feeling confused.

"How about if you stopped jerking around with all those other women?" Murphy barked at me. "That would show her how much you loved her, for starters."

"But nothing happened," I shot back at him. "I went in search of Sophie because I wanted to figure out what in the hell was going on in this new world we found ourselves in."

"You just don't get it, do you?" Murphy said, shaking his head slowly at me.

"Get what?" I said, exasperated.

"Why didn't you take Kiera with you? Why didn't you go with her and find out what was going on in this place? You're meant to be a team, aren't you? You're meant to be together. How do you think Kiera feels knowing that instead of trusting her to help out, you went running back to some old tart who gave you the boot years ago?"

"But..." I started, but Murphy was on a roll and wouldn't let me finish.

"The first time I met you, Potter, you were in the gutter," he said. "And it was that girl Sophie who put you there. She crushed your fucking heart without as much as a second thought. She treated you like a piece of dog shit. Once she realised what you were, she scraped you from the sole of her fucking boot. You meant nothing to her. She didn't respond to any of the letters you sent her, she didn't come looking for you – she did jack-shit!" Murphy stood up, his pipe gripped in his fist. Then pointing through the window in the direction of where Kiera's caravan was, he said, "Kiera's twice the woman than that Sophie ever was. You didn't see Kiera go running for the hills when she found out you were a Vampyrus. She did the exact opposite. Kiera came to you, helped you...loved you, and how have you repaid her? Huh? Fucked off back to your ex – that's how. And if that wasn't bad enough – the cherry on top of the cake – you then go and try to get your leg over with a freaking werewolf!"

"I didn't realise..." I started, no longer angry but scrambling for excuses.

"Whatever, Potter," Murphy snapped. "But one thing is for sure, if you want to get Kiera back, you need to man-up. Stop sitting there feeling sorry for yourself. Grow a fucking backbone and show that girl how much she means to you."

"But..." I started again.

"No buts, Potter!" he barked, jabbing his forefinger in the air. "The best thing that has ever happened to you is sitting alone just over there, and you're in here sulking like some fucking pre-teen." Then, looking hard at me with his crisp blue eyes, he added, "Women like Kiera come into the lives of men like us only once in a lifetime, Potter. If someone as special as Kiera loved me like I know how much she loves you, I wouldn't be sitting in here feeling sorry for myself. I'd be over there in her room on my hands and knees, begging for her fucking forgiveness."

I sat looking at Murphy and felt as if I'd had a verbal kick-in. I didn't know what to say. What could I say? Murphy was right.

"Don't throw away what you have with Kiera, Potter," he said, his voice now calmer. "Because if you do, you'll regret it for the rest of your sorry life. She is a good woman – she's precious. I wish I'd had with Pen, what you have with Kiera. You're a lucky man, Potter, but your problem is, you just don't see that."

Without saying another word, Murphy stepped inside the bedroom and closed the door.

Alone, I sat feeling almost stunned by what he had said. And only a true friend would have said what he had. Despite his piss-taking ways, I was not only lucky to have someone like Kiera in my life, I was lucky to have a friend like Murphy. Lying back on the sofa, I closed my eyes. I knew the situation I was now in with Kiera was of my own making. I'd been an idiot – a complete and utter nob-head. Murphy had been right; my loyalty to Sophie had been misplaced, she had never loved me like Kiera had. No one had ever come close to showing me the love I'd felt come from Kiera. It should have been Kiera I'd gone to for help – not Sophie. Kiera and I had been a team. *Had.* That word spoke of the past and it scared me. Would Kiera and I ever be a team again? I wondered, rolling onto my side.

Something dug into my thigh. I reached into my trouser pocket and my fingers touched something made of metal and glass. I pulled it out. I lay and stared at the iPod with the crescent moon on the back. I remembered taking it from the blazer pocket of Dorsey, who had died in my arms back in the barn. I suddenly had an idea. I hoped it would work.

Chapter Nine

Kiera

The caravan Murphy had duped the campsite owner into letting me use for the night was comfortable. There was a tiny electric heater attached to the wall and I switched it on. I peeled off the police coat, shirt, and trousers. They were damp from the snow. There was a chair, so I pulled it across the small room and draped my clothes over the back of it. I then positioned the chair in front of the fire to dry my clothes out. Naked, I went to the small bathroom. There was a toilet and shower in the closet-sized room. Good enough. I just wanted to feel clean again. I ran the water until steam was pouring from the showerhead and had covered the mirror fixed to the wall. There was a small complimentary bottle of shower gel and shampoo sitting in a soap dish attached to the shower wall.

I stood under the water and let it wash over my body. My skin tingled and my long, black hair clung to the sides of my face, shoulders, and back. Squeezing some of the shower gel into my hand, I looked for the first signs of those cracks again, but there weren't any. I guessed the blood from the wolves I had killed would still be working for me, but for how long, I didn't know. I hoped long enough for me to reach the Dead Waters.

With my fingertips, I worked the shampoo into my hair, and it smelt fresh and wonderful – a million miles away from the musty smell of the room where Jack had held me prisoner. I washed the dried werewolf blood from my arms, hands, and from in between my fingers. I just wanted to be rid of it. I turned off the water and stepped from the shower cubicle, grabbing a towel from a rail fixed to the wall. Wrapping it around me, I wiped the steam from the mirror and stared at my reflection. I looked into the eyes that stared back at me, and I somehow felt as if I were looking into the soul of a stranger. Those fine streaks of hazel around the edges of my pupils flashed orange like the rays of a hot sun. I opened my mouth and let my fangs protrude from my gums. Then, slowly I raised my hands and released my long, black claws. Rolling back my shoulders, I let the towel drop to the floor. Standing naked before the mirror, my wings sprang from my back like two giant sails unfurling. There was little room for them in the small bathroom, and they pressed flat against the shower cubicle behind me. The claws at each tip opened and closed slowly, as if grabbing hold of air. I looked at myself, knowing that this was only the second occasion I had ever taken the time to truly study myself – get to know what I truly was. My skin was paper white in utter contrast to my long, black wings and claws. In my half-breed form, my hair was more navy blue than black.

Even before I'd truly had a chance to come to terms with the realisation that I was only half human, I had suddenly learnt I wasn't half human at all. I was a half and half – half Vampyrus and half wolf. What did that make me? A freak – that's what it made me. I was an abomination! I was born of a forbidden act. I was the result of a forbidden love affair between something close to a bat and a wolf. The Elders were right – such a creature like me shouldn't be alive. Nature knew it, too – that's why others like me – including Murphy's daughters – had withered away, left to cling to life in some makeshift hospital hidden in the attic at Hallowed Manor.

Somehow the Dead Waters had saved me. They had brought me back to life. But why? What was the purpose? Was it so I could be tormented? Made to suffer? Or was there another reason? The Elders had said I'd been chosen to choose between the humans and the Vampyrus – only one race could survive. But there was a third race – the *Lycanthrope*. Even if I had chosen between the humans and the Vampyrus, there would have still been two races left – the second being the Lycanthrope. What about them? Did the Elders have any idea what I truly was? Or had Murphy covered his tracks so well, that they still believed me to be a half-breed? I doubted they knew my true heritage. If they did, I'd be dead already, and so would Murphy. I looked at myself once more, then making a fist with my hand, I smashed it into the mirror. The glass fractured, distorting my face into a million different pieces. Blood trickled from between my knuckles and I licked them clean.

I stepped away from the mirror. With my wings trailing behind me, I walked into what was the living room of the caravan. My clothes were still drying by the electric heater. I stood in the centre of the poky room and let my wings open on either side of me. In a strange way, I felt a certain kind of freedom being naked and in my true form. It was like I was no longer hiding what I truly was behind clothes, secrets, and lies. This was me – wings, claws, fangs and all. And what about the wolf inside of me? I didn't know how I felt about that. Did it make a difference? It had always been there, right? I had just never known about it. But there was a part of me – somewhere down in the basement – which feared it.

Wanting to totally feel free, I took the coat from the chair and reached inside the pockets. They were empty.

"Where is it?" I fretted out loud. "Where is my iPod?"

I threw the coat to one side and checked the trouser pockets. Nothing. Then taking a deep breath, I realised I must have left my iPod in my other coat pocket – the coat that I had stuffed under the seat at the back of the police van. The police van that was now a day's drive away.

I couldn't go on without it. I would be lost without music. I needed those songs to listen to when I couldn't sleep, when I felt unhappy, when I tried to make sense of each new day. I had to go back for it. I would fly if I had to. But what if I started to crack up again? What if I fell out of the sky like I had done before? Potter and Murphy wouldn't know where to find me. I would tell them then.

"They're not going to agree to go all the way back there," I muttered, starting to feel panicked. "That place would be swarming with Skin-walkers by now. Murphy would say it was too dangerous."

I looked at my claws, touched my face, and checked the flat of my stomach for any signs of those cracks. There weren't any – but that didn't mean they wouldn't return at any time. I couldn't risk dropping out of the sky like a stone. But I had to go back. I had to risk it. Turning, I reached for the door and opened it and gasped out loud. Potter was standing in the darkness outside my door.

"Where are you sneaking off to?" Potter asked.

Chapter Ten

Potter

Kiera stood in the open doorway. The dull light from within the caravan made her wings sparkle as if showered with glitter. She looked breathtakingly beautiful – like a dark angel standing before me. Her thick, dark hair shone blue, her pale skin like perfectly smooth marble, and her breasts so pert I could have hung my coat from them. The last time I had seen her look like this was when we had made love in the summerhouse back at Hallowed Manor. I just wanted to hold her in my arms again, to feel her soft skin and wings against mine. I desperately wanted for both of us to be together in our true form. Whatever Kiera truly was, half-breed, half and half, there was no mistaking she was the most beautiful creature I had ever seen.

Fighting my first instinct to race up the steps and hold her in my arms, I took a deep breath and said, "Where are you going?"

"Nowhere important," she said.

"So unimportant you forgot to put your clothes on and hide your wings?" I half-smiled at her.

Realising she was standing naked in the doorway, Kiera gasped, letting her wings fold about her like a blanket. She stepped back inside. I climbed the steps, entered the caravan, and closed the door behind me.

"Did I invite you in?" she asked, standing before me, now hidden beneath her wings.

"I just wanted to talk, Kiera," I said.

"Look, I don't have time to talk now," she said impatiently. "It will have to wait until tomorrow.

"What do you mean you don't have time?" I asked with a frown, sensing that she wanted rid of me. "What else have you got planned in the middle of nowhere?"

"If you must know, I left my iPod back at the van and I'm going to go get it," she said, staring at me.

"Have you lost your mind?" I asked, not wanting to sound belittling in anyway. I knew how important her iPod was to her.

"I can't go on without it," she said, a desperate look in her eyes. "I need it back."

"You can't, Kiera, that place will be swarming with wolves by now," I tried to convince her.

Looking close to tears, Kiera said, "But I'm lost without being able to listen to music."

I put my hand in my pocket and wondered if for once I hadn't been cut a break. I had planned to use the iPod I had found to hopefully woo Kiera back, but this turn of events was working out far better than I could have ever imagined.

Slowly, I took my hand from my pocket and said, "You don't have to feel lost anymore, Kiera." I uncurled my fist to reveal the iPod.

Kiera looked down at it then back at me. "Where did you get that?" she breathed.

"The wolf-boy who helped set me up with that teacher, Emily Clarke, had it. He used FaceTime on it so you could see me with her," I explained, offering it to Kiera.

Slowly, Kiera reached out and took it from me. She turned it over and over in her hands. She dragged the tip of one claw over the crescent moon logo on the back of it.

"There weren't any songs on it," I told her. "So I downloaded one for you."

Kiera looked at me. "Really? What song?"

"Listen to it when I'm gone," I said, fighting the urge to break her stare. I was never very good at this sort of thing. But I kept hearing Murphy's gruff, angry voice in my ears. "The song says how I feel."

"About what?" Kiera pushed.

"You," I said back.

"Why can't you say it?" Kiera asked.

"Because I don't know how many ways I can say I'm sorry to you for what I've done," I started to explain. "Murphy says words aren't good enough. He said I have to show you, but I don't know how, Kiera."

"You've spoken to Murphy about us?" Kiera asked, sounding cross.

"No, he spoke to me about us," I said. "I guess he was sick of seeing me wandering around like a tit in a trance."

"What did he tell you?" Kiera asked, some of the frostiness leaving her voice.

"The truth," I said, looking straight back at her. "It was only what I already knew in my heart, but was too arrogant to admit. I haven't treated you right, Kiera, and I'm ashamed of that. But although I've hurt you, I never meant to. That was the last thing I wanted to do."

"And what about now?" Kiera asked, her voice soft like a whisper.

"What do you mean?" I said.

"Now that you know I'm half wolf – doesn't that change how you feel about me?" she asked, her voice sounding kind of scared. "I know how much you hate wolves."

"But I don't hate you," I tried to convince her.

"I'm not who you thought I was," Kiera said, a single tear spilling onto her cheek and sliding slowly down her face.

I wanted to go to her, but I stopped myself. I didn't know if she was ready to be held by me just yet – if ever again.

"I was stupid to have given you my heart," Kiera whispered.

"Don't say that," I said, I couldn't bear it. "Never say that, Kiera."

"Why not?" she asked, arming away that single tear from her chin.

"Because I couldn't give a crap if you were half toad and half orangutan, I would love you all the same," I desperately tried to convince her. "I might not have a heart anymore, Kiera, but it aches all the same to see you so sad. I'm so sorry for how I have treated you."

Kiera looked at me, her face now streaked with silent tears. "You think you can come in here and say all the right words and it will make it all better? It doesn't work like that," she whispered.

"Why not?" I asked.

"Because I'm scared," she said.

"Of what?"

"Of giving you everything, only for you to hurt me again," Kiera said, choking back her tears.

"But I'm scared, too," I told her.

"What have you got to be scared of?" she asked me, her wings gleaming black and folded tightly around her like a shield.

"Of never being able to hold you again," I confessed. "I'm so fucking scared, Kiera, I might have to spend the rest of my life without you being the most beautiful part of it. Over the years I've been hunted, chased, beaten, even murdered, but nothing has made me feel as scared as I do now. I should have known better than to break your heart. But it's done now and I don't know how to mend it."

Slowly, I turned away. I couldn't bear to look upon her tear-stained face anymore, knowing it was me who had made her cry. I opened the door, stepped back out into the night and left Kiera alone.

Chapter Eleven

Kiera

With my wings still folded around me, I went to the bedroom and lay down on the bed. I drew my knees against my chest beneath my wings. My body shook with sobs. Half of me wanted to go to the door and call Potter back. I wanted to take him beneath my wings and let him make love to me. But the other half of me, the half that was scared of the hurt that being in love could bring, refused to give me the courage to go after him, however much I wanted to.

As if my wings were a blanket, I hid beneath them, too scared to come out again. Being in love with Potter was so hard. It was like an obsession, and that's what I truly feared. I knew I would never stop loving him, but that just opened me up to a world full of hurt. That's what guys like Potter brought to the party. But I couldn't imagine my life without him. My feelings for him hadn't really changed. If I searched them, I knew I had fallen in love with him the moment he had opened his arrogant mouth and called me Miss Marple. Luke had been nothing more than a distraction for me – a Band-Aid temporarily holding back the flood of feelings I secretly had for Potter. Potter had always been the man I had wanted. And I still wanted him now – the pain he had caused me hadn't changed that. I hated myself for feeling how I did. So why didn't I just take him back? Because I knew Potter wasn't mine to have. He was Sophie's – he always had been, and always would be. The Elders had told me I wouldn't go back with the others. This was a one-way trip for me. They had shown me those statues of my friends. I had seen Isidor with Melody, Murphy with his daughters, Kayla with Sam, and Potter with Sophie.

Ultimately, they were going to be together. Not in this *pushed* world, but the one they were going back to when I put this mess right.

So however much my body ached for Potter, I knew, just like I had fought my cravings for the human red stuff in the zoo, if I gave in to them, it would only lead me down a nightmarish road of despair. However hard it was for me, I had to let go of Potter – he wasn't mine to take. I could give in and be happy with him again for a time, but that would be selfish of me. My friends would never go home; they would never get the chance of being together again. I wanted that for them. The hardest thing for me to do was to give away the man I loved to another, but harder still would be to see my friends unhappy.

Deep down, I knew I couldn't really hate Potter for going in search of Sophie again. It just proved to me, just like the Elders had said, they were meant to be together. Did he *really* choose to go in search of Sophie? Or was it just the world trying to *push* itself back into place again? Potter just didn't realise that yet.

Beneath my wings, I uncurled my claws from around the iPod that Potter had given to me. I pressed the 'Music' icon. Just like Potter had said, there was only one song downloaded onto it. It was the song Potter had chosen for me. I slowly unwound the earphones that had been wrapped around the bottom of the iPod and pressed them into my ears. With my eyes shut tight to stop the on flood of tears, I listened to 'Annie's Song' by John Denver.

With the song set on repeat, I listened to the words of that song, which Potter had so carefully chosen. The music spoke of forests. In my sleepy mind I pictured the secret forest we were heading to and the Dead Waters which were hidden there. John Denver sung about mountains and I could see them in my mind. The peaks were dusted white with snow. Set between the mountains there was a small town. The streets were narrow and cobbled. I had been there before...

Chapter Twelve

Kiera

...I made my way through the throng of people who crushed themselves in the town centre. There was a fountain, and I'd seen it before. I had been here with Kayla and Isidor after escaping that zoo. I was once again in the town of Wasp Water.

Tudor-style houses lined each side of the narrow streets. People leant out of the upper windows, all looking in the direction of the town square. What was drawing their attention to it? What were they so desperate to see? The others crowding the narrow streets were just like me. All of them had bright hazel eyes, which burned in their sockets. All of them were wolves. I blended in with them. None of them knew they were being infiltrated by me.

I wedged my slender frame through the crowds, slipping beneath waving arms, and between bustling bodies. The crowd buzzed with an excitable current, and in the distance I could hear a voice bellowing through a loudhailer. The voice sounded hissy and broken. But it stirred the crowds, bringing them to a feverish excitement. Desperate to find out what was causing such elation, I forced my way into the town square. The fountain had been reduced to rubble, and in its place had been erected what looked like a raised wooden stage. In the middle of this there was a guillotine. It stood tall, its silver blade gleaming in the morning light. Dried blood covered the edge of it, the sides, and the floor of the wooden structure. Before the guillotine sat a large metal bucket. It was then I understood why the crowds of wolves were so excited; they had gathered to witness an execution.

I glanced left and right at their human-looking faces. But they were not really human; they just hid beneath human skin.

They were Skin-walkers. With my eyes as yellow as theirs, I looked just like one of them. They did not suspect there was a traitor amongst their number. I looked back at the stage.

There was a man standing to the right, a loudspeaker pressed to his lips.

"Okay, my friends, please get ready for today's main event!" he roared through the speaker. His voice sounded broken and high-pitched.

The crowd whooped and punched the air.

"Please welcome to the stage, our executioner!"

The crowd erupted again, whistled and cheered as a hooded man stepped onto the stage from the right. His black mask had two narrow slits cut in the front. I could see his eyes blazing out of those two holes like headlamps. He waved at the crowed as they waved back at him. I looked over my shoulder. There was a sea of arms waving back and forth in the air. I looked back at the stage. The guy with the speaker spoke into it again and said, "So who are you going to be beheading for us today?"

"A killer!" the executioner roared at the crowd from beneath his hood. "A killer of wolves!"

The crowd roared angrily, punching the air with their fists.

"But he is not just a killer of wolves, this man is a traitor, too!" the executioner barked, whipping the crowd into a frenzy.

The Skin-walkers hissed and booed.

"He is one of us, but has deceived us all!" the guy with the speaker almost screeched. The loudhailer made an ear-splitting whining sound and I covered my ears.

"Kill him! Kill him! Kill him!" the crowd started to chant.

Who was this traitor the crowd so wanted to see beheaded? I wondered. Then, from the right, another hooded man was shoved onto the stage. Unlike the executioner, this man didn't have eye slits cut into his mask. He staggered blindly across the stage. His arms were secured behind his back with chains. The executioner grabbed him roughly by the arm.

"Unmask him!" someone roared from the crowd.

"Show us the traitor's face!" another yelled.

"Unmask him! Unmask him! Unmask him!" the crowd wailed as one.

The guy with the speaker teased the audience by shouting, "What was that? I can't hear you!"

"UNMASK HIM! UNMASK HIM! UNMASK HIM!" they now screamed.

Like a magician pulling a rabbit out of a hat, the guy with the speaker stepped forward and whipped off the prisoner's hood.

I looked in shock at my brother's emaciated face. Jack Seth looked defiantly at the crowd.

"KILL HIM!" the crowd cried.

Then, from somewhere deep in the audience pressed into the town square, what looked like a big red tomato was hurled at Jack. It splattered into his chest, and ran in a thick, red stream down the front of his denim shirt. Once one item had been thrown, more followed. Jack's face and body became covered in red... red... oh, my God... the crowd was throwing human body parts at him! I looked to my right and watched in horror as the Skin-walker standing next to me produced a severed human hand from a carrier bag he was holding. He hurled it at the stage. I watched it fly through the air like a giant flesh coloured spider with five legs. The hand slapped against Jack's face, leaving a bloody red handprint behind.

"Hey, you haven't brought anything to throw?" the Skin-walker with the carrier bag said.

I looked at him, desperate to hide my revulsion, so as not to give myself away.

"I've got plenty of stuff in here if you want something to throw," he smiled, waving the bag in front of my face. "I've got fingers and toes. There are two hearts in here someplace, and some brain. Brain is always good at these events – it sticks so well!"

"No thanks," I said, turning away, fighting the urge to puke my guts up.

"Suit yourself," the Skin-walker said, reaching into his bag and pulling out a human eyeball. He then tossed it at the stage towards my brother.

Jack stood defiantly. Even though his entire face and body dripped red with blood, guts, and body tissue, he stood with his back straight, face turned towards the crowd. A severed foot shot overhead and smashed into the side of his face. His head rocked momentarily to the left.

"Now that was really a kick in the head!" the guy with the speaker yelled.

The crowd roared with laughter. When they had run out of human remains to hurl at Jack, the executioner shoved him back across the stage towards the guillotine.

"Off with his head!" a Skin-walker screeched from behind me.

With his hands manacled behind his back, Jack could offer no resistance. The executioner made a swiping kick at Jack's long legs. They buckled beneath him. He sprawled onto the stage, and the executioner forced Jack's head beneath the guillotine.

Why were they doing this to him? Jack was one of them. I edged myself closer to the stage. I had to save him, but how? I was one against five hundred or more. Still I started to push myself closer to the stage. But there were just too many people. I pushed harder, desperate now to save Jack's life. But I just couldn't reach him. The stage didn't seem to be getting any nearer.

"Take off his head!" another of the Skin-walkers whooped.

They then began to chant over and over. I pushed and shoved my way through the crowd. I reached the stage as Jack suddenly looked up. Our eyes met. His were bright and spinning.

"I love you, sister," he whispered.

There was a sound of metal slicing against wood as the blade dropped at speed. Throwing my hands to my face, I watched Jack's head drop into the bucket before him.

Chapter Thirteen

Potter

"Wake up!" a gruff sounding voice bellowed in my ear.

I opened my eyes to find Murphy peering at me through a haze of blue pipe smoke. It smelt pungent, making my eyes water.

"I'm glad to see the little chat we had last night worked," he grunted.

"What are you talking about?" I groaned, swinging my legs over the side of the sofa and planting my feet on the floor.

"I can see you've been lying there all night, crying your eyes out," he said, shoving a mug of strong black coffee into my hands.

"I'm not crying," I said. "It's that fucking thing you have constantly dangling from the corner of your mouth. The smoke is making my eyes water."

"Bollocks," Murphy said, turning away and heading back towards the kitchenette. "You're nothing but a big girl's blouse."

"Look, I'm really not in the mood for your theatrics this morning," I sighed, squinting at him through the trail of pipe smoke he had left behind. "I went and saw Kiera last night."

"It didn't go well, then," Murphy said, pouring himself a mug of coffee.

"How do you know?" I asked.

"You're sleeping on the couch, aren't ya?" he said with a grin.

"I'm glad that the fact my life is in fucking ruins amuses you," I said, looking down at the mug of coffee and taking a sip. My throat still felt sore. I looked at my trembling hands as they gripped the mug of coffee. The cracks were back, like faint, watery veins beneath the skin, but they were there.

Slowly, Murphy came back towards me, and leaning against the wall by the door, he said, "Okay, I'm sorry, Potter. What really happened?"

"Not a lot really," I said with a shrug. The room felt cold. My coat was on the floor so I put it on, covering my bare chest and arms. Then reaching into the pocket, I pulled the last bottle of Lot-13 out. "I think I've truly blown it this time."

"You don't know that for sure," Murphy tried to say in his own unique way to comfort me. "Look at it like this, Kiera is still here, isn't she? She hasn't split on you."

"She's only tagging along in the hopes we will find Kayla and Sam," I said, unscrewing the bottle cap. "Once we've reached the Dead Waters, I think she'll be gone."

"We'll see," Murphy said thoughtfully. "Perhaps I could talk to her for you?"

"No thanks," I said, tilting my head back and taking a gulp of the red stuff. It tasted bitter and I grimaced. I handed the bottle to Murphy.

"Why don't you want me to talk to her for you?" Murphy asked.

"Because somewhere deep inside of me, I hope there is a chance, however remote, that we might get back together. I don't want you fucking things up for me," I said, pulling back the curtain, peering out of the caravan window.

"Thanks," Murphy grunted, then drank from the bottle.

"Save some for Kiera," I reminded him.

Murphy took the bottle from his lips, and replaced the cap. A third of the gloopy-looking stuff sloshed around the bottom of the bottle. I took it from him and placed it back into my pocket. "So what's the plan, Sarge?"

"We head for the Dead Waters," Murphy explained. "If the snow holds off, we could make it by nightfall. Some of those mountain passes are going to be treacherous, so our progress is going to be slow in places."

"Couldn't we just fly?" I asked.

"You know it's too risky," he said. "We're all slowly cracking up. Flying could be dangerous."

"Any more dangerous than navigating those roads in the snow?" I said, looking back out of the window at the snow-covered world beyond it.

"It's not just the cracks that bother me," Murphy said, puffing thoughtfully on his pipe.

"What then?" I quizzed, taking a cigarette from my pocket and lighting it. A thick fog of smoke settled over the room like a low-flying cloud.

"The statues," he said, looking at me through the smog. "I think they're following us. I think they always have been, ever since we got *pushed* here."

"Even more reason to up, up, and away then," I said.

"No," Murphy grumbled. "I think, like us, they are trying to get to the Dead Waters. I think that's why they are following us."

"What are they?" I asked.

"I don't know," he said. "But I've taken a good, close-up look once or twice, and although they are as solid as a pervert's hard-on, I think there is a living soul inside."

"Kiera thought she saw one of them move," I told him, taking down a throat full of smoke.

"Where?" Murphy asked, sounding startled.

"Back at Hallowed Manor," I explained.

"What did this statue look like?"

"A statue," I shrugged.

"I know it looked like a fucking statue!" Murphy barked. "What kind of statue? Male? Female? Vampyrus...?"

"A girl," I said.

"A girl?" Murphy said, fixing me with a hard stare. But it was like he was looking through me rather than at me.

"Kayla said she was chased by one on the grounds of Ravenwood School," I continued.

"Another girl?" Murphy pushed.

"No, a boy, I think," I told him.

Murphy looked slightly disappointed on hearing this. It was like he had a secret theory about the statues, and by me telling him that one of them had been a boy, it had shattered his beliefs somehow.

"What are you thinking?" I asked.

"We don't fly," he said, looking at me. "We drive and take it slow. If my hunch is right, then we don't want to leave any of the statues behind."

"Why not?"

He didn't answer. Murphy pulled open the caravan door and headed outside. I followed him to the doorway then stopped. Way off in the distance, I could see Kiera heading out across the field which stretched away at the back of the campsite. Her head was bowed low against the wind, her hands thrust into her coat pockets. I knew at once she was looking for an animal – she was going in search of some of the red stuff. As I stood and watched her, I had a sudden idea. I would have to be quick. Working fast, like a blaze of shadows, I put my plan into action.

Chapter Fourteen

Kiera

I had been up early. I had hardly slept at all. What little snippets of sleep I had managed to find, had been haunted by Potter. So I gave up with the idea of sleeping and had got up at first light. I had taken the opportunity of having another shower, and once dressed, had left my caravan. Just like it had been for days, there was a chill wind, but it had stopped snowing at last. With my hair blowing about my face, and my hands thrust into my coat pockets, I headed towards a small, wooded area which circled the land at the far corner of the campsite. The skin covering the backs of my hands, arms, shoulders, and back had started to crack again. My flesh felt taut and brittle. I knew that if I didn't get hold of some red stuff, and soon, it would only be an hour or two before I completely turned to stone. I knew there was only one bottle of Lot-13 left in Potter's pocket. I wouldn't go to him for it. Not because I was stubborn or didn't want his help, but why should I have it? Wasn't his need as great as mine?

As I had lain curled beneath my wings during the night, I had decided that I would no longer fight with Potter. I wanted the little time we had together to be happy – not fraught with bad feelings and tension. We wouldn't be lovers again, but we could be friends. So I wouldn't put upon him, I would find some of the red stuff for myself. Reaching the treeline, I knew I could easily find a squirrel, muntjac, or rat to feed on. It wasn't ideal, but it was better than feeding on a human. I would never do that.

"Are you looking for some of this?" I heard a voice say.

I turned around to find Potter standing amongst the trees. He was holding up a bottle of Lot-13. I could see that it was a third full.

"It's all we have left, but I saved the last for you," he said.

Although I felt the sudden urge to run to him, snatch it from his hands, and swallow down the last of the thick, sticky liquid, I stopped myself and said, "It's okay, I can find some of the red stuff for myself. You have it – you need it as much as I do."

"Suit yourself," Potter said, unscrewing the cap.

I watched him lift the bottle to his mouth and drink the last of it. He tossed the empty bottle into the undergrowth as he stood in a shaft of white sunlight which cut through the branches high above. The tails of his long black coat flapped about his legs. The coat was open down the front, revealing his naked upper body. I looked away.

There must be some kind of woodland animal nearby. I tried to focus, set my senses straight, but with Potter standing only feet away, I just couldn't concentrate.

"Did you listen to the song?" he asked, taking a step closer to me.

"Yes," I whispered, continuing with the pretence that I was looking for food. "It was nice."

"Just nice?" he asked, edging his way closer, the sound of his feet crunching over broken twigs seemed almost deafening.

"It was *nice*," I said again. What did he want me to say? Did he want me to tell him I'd spent the night crying my eyes out at the thought of him being in the arms of Sophie? Is that what he wanted to hear? Did he want me to tell him how the words of that song had broken my heart? I couldn't tell him that.

"So is it over between us?" Potter asked, his voice suddenly so close I could feel his warm breath against my cheek.

I shuddered. "It has to be," I whispered.

"It can't be over," he said, so close now that I could feel him brushing against my back.

"Why not?" I breathed, scared of turning to face him.

"We never had that date we always dreamt about," he whispered into my ear.

"It's too late for that now," I said softly.

"Come with me," he said, taking my hand gently in his and guiding me deeper into the woods.

"Where are you taking me?" I asked, letting him lead me away.

Without saying a word, Potter led me into a small, open area surrounded by tall pine trees. I couldn't help but gasp with delight. In the middle was a tree stump. On this, there was a glass, which had been filled with a fistful of wild woodland flowers. I could see beautiful white snowdrops, star-shaped flowers coloured blue and mauve, and bunches of sweet violet. There was one more glass and this was filled with a deep red liquid which looked like wine. A blanket had been laid over the snow before the tree stump.

"It's not much, I know," Potter said, leading me into the secluded patch. "But it's the closest I could get to a date in the middle of nowhere and at such short notice."

"It's wonderful," I murmured as he guided me down onto the blanket. "Where did you get all of this from?"

"The glasses I took from the kitchen in the caravan, the flowers I found nearby."

"And the red stuff?" I asked, looking at the glass of blood.

"That came from me," he said, covering a small open wound on his wrist with the sleeve of his coat.

My stomach summersaulted at seeing the glass of blood within my reach. My throat burnt and went dry.

"A date isn't a proper date without some music," he said, holding out his hand."

I took the iPod from my pocket and handed it to him. He pressed the screen with his thumb as he downloaded tracks. I looked at the glass of his blood again, my stomach cramping. Potter placed the iPod on the tree stump next to the glass of flowers. The song *When I Was Your Man* by Bruno Mars filled the small enclosure. Potter could see me staring at the glass of his blood.

"I can't drink it," I whispered, unable to take my eyes off the glass.

"Why not?" he asked softly.

"Because I can't have you," I said, turning to look at him. "You're not mine to take."

"I am," he said over the soft sound of the music.

"You belong to Sophie," I whispered. "The Elders showed me."

"What do you mean?" Potter said, startled.

I looked at him and said, "They showed me a statue of you and a woman. You both looked really happy together. You looked in love. But that woman wasn't me, Potter. It was Sophie. The Elders said it is her you will be with."

"And you really believe a single word those twisted fucks say?" he asked me.

"Why not?" I said, taking my eyes from the glass and looking at him.

"Because they are fucking with us," Potter said. "Can't you see that? This whole *pushed* world – the fact they've brought us back – is to punish you for not making that decision.

77

They know how much you care for your friends; that's why we've all been brought back too – so you can see us suffer. But more than that, they know how you feel about me. What better way to hurt you than tell you it's Sophie I'm going to end up with?"

"But what if they are telling the truth?" I said, not wanting to have false hope for fear of being hurt.

"They're lying," Potter insisted.

"How can you be so sure?" I asked him.

"Because I know how much I love you, Kiera," he said, taking my hands in his. "I love you so much. More than I have ever loved anyone. How many ways have I got to tell you that?"

"But what if we love each other only to find out that the Elders are right?" I said, looking into his jet-black eyes. "I don't think I could bear losing you all over again."

"It's my choice who I want to spend the rest of my life with," Potter said. "And I chose to spend it with you, Kiera, not Sophie. It's you I want. It's you I've always wanted."

"But you don't understand," I said, tears burning at the corners of my eyes. "I won't be coming back with you, Potter. I have to stay here."

"Then, I'll stay with you," he said, gripping my hands tighter in his, as the music continued to sweep all about us.

"If you stay, then I think you'll die," I whispered through my flowing tears. "You'll die just like me."

"If I can't be with you, Kiera, I would rather be dead," he said, pulling me close. "My life has no meaning without you in it. I'm not going back without you, and that's a promise. We live together or not at all." Slowly, Potter gently placed his lips over mine and kissed me. I kissed him back.

Chapter Fifteen

Kiera

Pushing me gently down onto the blanket, Potter covered my neck in kisses, which were so gentle and tender, it felt as if my skin were being caressed with a feather. With my eyes closed, I ran my fingers through his hair and pulled him down on top of me.

"I love you, Kiera," he murmured between kisses.

"I love you, too," I said. I couldn't lie or hide my feelings for him. I had never stopped loving him.

Slowly, we peeled each other's clothes away, casting them aside so we were free of them. Potter arched his back, releasing his wings in a fine spray of black shadows. Naked, he knelt over me, leaning down to cover my breasts in kisses. My wings unfolded beneath me like a soft bed of feathers. I wrapped my arms around his back and held him. Turning his attention from my breasts, Potter kissed my mouth again. Locked in each other's arms, we floated up into the air above the secret clearing. With our wings rippling gently in the wind on either side, we turned slowly around and around in the air like two angels dancing. The song *The Power of Love* by Gabrielle Aplin filtered up from below. We turned slowly, around and around, locked in each other's arms, our wings beating softly like a heartbeat. Snow fell from the branches of the nearby trees, swirling through the air, glittering in the early morning light like falling stars. We kissed each other slowly, our tongues locked together like our arms and legs. I felt Potter ease himself gently inside of me, truly making us one. I shuddered with pleasure, groaning out loud as we continued to turn in the air just above the secluded spot. Hidden by the trees, it felt as if we were the only people alive in this *pushed* world.

Opening his eyes, Potter looked into mine and said, "I'll never leave you again, Kiera. It is you who I want to be with, not another."

Kissing me again, we slowly dropped out of the sky, landing softly on the blanket. Hidden beneath our wings, Potter slowly eased himself in and out of me. I drew my knees up and arched my back, as he worked his strong hips up and down. I ran my claws up and down the length of his back. He moaned as my sharp nails pierced his skin. The sudden smell of his blood heightened my desire for him. I broke our kiss, as my fangs slid from my gums. He looked down at me and smiled, his fangs glistening wetly just inches from my face. Without saying a word, he tilted his head to the right, offering his neck to me. Jerking my head forward, I nipped at his skin, the smell of his blood racing through his veins turning me wild. Unable to resist him or his blood for one more moment, I sank my teeth into his flesh. Potter's blood gushed into my mouth. It was hot, and hit the back of my throat like a shot of strong whiskey. I ravenously sucked at the wound I had opened in his neck. His blood pumped into my mouth in thick, sticky waves. A warm sensation fanned out inside of me, across my chest, stomach, and between my legs.

Potter moved faster and faster above me, his breathing getting deeper and quicker with every thrust of his hips. With his blood running from the corners of my mouth, I pulled my lips away, gripping his arse and clawing him deeper into me. I threw my head back against the blanket, as Potter sank his teeth into my neck. I felt a sudden burning sensation as my skin broke. With a seething excitement flowing open in the pit of my stomach, I let him feed off me, as he pushed into me faster and faster. With my head feeling light and my skin tingling, a warm, throbbing pulse flooded through my entire being as a swell of unimaginable desire erupted deep within me. I cried out, wrapping my legs about his back, keeping Potter locked deep inside of me as my body trembled and rocked.

Potter withdrew his fangs from my neck and cried out, as he jerked inside of me. Then, just when I thought he was going to collapse, spent and out of breath above me, he suddenly picked me up in a burst of energy and threw me into the air. With my wings fluttering, I crashed into the trunk of a nearby tree. Snow showered down, as Potter lunged at me. I grabbed for him with my claws, fangs on show.

"I want you so fucking bad," he snarled, his wings pointing out behind him, fangs razor-sharp and protruding from his gums like white daggers.

"Take me again, then," I hissed, raking my claws up his back and over his shoulders.

Gripping my thighs with his powerful claws, Potter pushed me back and up against the tree. Once inside of me again, he wasted no time in building up to a frantic rhythm. With my eyes half opened, I looked down into his face, and it was the first time while making love, I think we had both truly given in to the animal instincts deep inside of us. I was no longer scared of those feelings; I gave in to them. I gave in to Potter and he gave in to me.

Snarling at him, I pushed him backwards. He flew across the clearing, landing on his back. A wake of snow shot up into the air. Even before it had settled again, I was on him. With my wings arched high, shielding us from the rest of the world, I slid down on top of him. Potter grabbed my breasts, my throat, anything he could get hold of. He pulled me forward, covering me in kisses. He nipped at my flesh with his fangs and I groaned with pleasure. I moved up and down, and when I felt the muscles in his stomach and thighs contract, I pushed myself fully down onto him. Potter arched his back and cried out as if it was an involuntary act – something he could neither control nor keep locked inside. A fiery hot gush of pleasure suddenly gripped me, making my whole body shake like I was undergoing some violent seizure. With tears of sweat covering my body in a silky gloss, I collapsed into Potter's welcoming arms.

He pulled me down on top of him. Still inside of me, Potter held me tight and breathed, "I want us to stay locked together like this forever. I never want to be apart from you again, tiger."

"We feel like one person," I whispered, still trying to catch my breath.

"I don't ever want that feeling to go away," he said, stroking a stray length of hair from my brow.

"Nor do I," I whispered, resting my head against his chest. But in my head, I could still see that statue of Potter and Sophie looking so happy together. "Hold me tight," I said.

"For always," he whispered back, folding his wings over us like a blanket.

Chapter Sixteen

Potter

"We should get going," I whispered in Kiera's ear.

"So soon?" she murmured against my chest. "I could stay here with you like this forever.

I pulled my wings tight about us. "Me too, but Murphy is going to be sorely pissed if we keep him waiting much longer."

"I guess you're right, but..." Kiera trailed off.

"But what?" I whispered.

"Once we leave here, things are going to change," she said. "I get the feeling that we're coming to the end of our journey in this *pushed* world. I get the feeling that everyone will continue on from here, while I'm being led down a dead end."

"I won't leave you here," I said. "If you stay, I stay. We're like a pair, a team. We're like a couple of old bookends."

"Not so much of the old," Kiera grinned up at me, slapping my stomach with the palm of her hand.

"C'mon, we should start heading back," I said, unfurling my wings.

We dressed without speaking. The glass of my blood stood on the tree stump next to the flowers. It had gone thick and black like treacle. I hooked it out with my finger. The congealed lump splattered to the ground, turning the snow pink.

"Ready?" I asked, looking over my shoulder at Kiera.

"All set," she smiled, pulling her coat tightly about her slender frame.

Reaching out, I took her hand in mine and led her back through the wooded area and towards the field. At the treeline,

I could see the row of caravans in the distance. "C'mon," I said, heading back across the field towards them.

Murphy was waiting. He stood propped against the bonnet of the car, pipe dangling unlit from the corner of his mouth. He looked at how Kiera now had her arm hooked through mine. Before he'd had the chance to say anything, the campsite owner appeared from around the side of the kiosk. He had a spanner in his hand and I guessed he had been fixing the broken cigarette machine.

"Found him then?" he said, looking at Kiera.

"Huh?" Kiera asked.

"Your friend here," he said, nodding in Murphy's direction, "has just been telling me how Gabriel often wanders off and gets himself lost."

Cheeky bastard, I thought, glancing at Murphy. He simply shrugged his thickset shoulders at me.

"That's right," Kiera agreed with the campsite owner. Doing her best to hide a smile, she looked up at me and said, "Gabriel was lost, but I've found him again now."

The campsite owner came towards me. Then, talking as if I wasn't there at all, he sighed and said, "Poor fella. In the daylight, I can see he ain't exactly normal. He's got that vacant look behind the eyes. I can tell he's not too tightly wrapped." Then, reaching into his trouser pocket, he produced a bar of chocolate. "Go on, son, take it. It's a little treat. I'm sure your social worker won't mind me giving it to you. It is okay if I give him some chocolate, ain't it?" he said, glancing at Kiera.

"Sure," Kiera smiled. "Take the chocolate from the nice man, *Gabe.*"

"You're enjoying this aren't you?" I growled at her. Turning to face the campsite owner, I added, "You can stick your chocolate bar right up your fu..."

84

"We should be going," Murphy suddenly cut in. "Gabriel is starting to get upset again."

"I think you're right," Kiera said, guiding me by the arm towards the car. "Say goodbye to the nice man."

"The nice man can go fu…" I started to say.

"Thank you for the use of your caravans," Murphy said, cutting over me and approaching the man. He took hold of his hand and pumped it up and down.

"You're welcome," the owner said, glancing over Murphy's shoulder as Kiera shoved me onto the backseat of the car. "Perhaps you could give this to him later, when he's calmed down a bit."

"Sure," Murphy smiled, taking the chocolate bar. "I'm sure he'll love it."

Turning, Murphy made his way back to the car and climbed in. Kiera jumped in next to him and slammed the door shut. Not wanting to waste another minute, Murphy shoved the car into reverse and steered it back down the lane and towards the road. The tyres crunched over the snow as the car lurched left then right. The campsite owner watched us go, then headed back towards the kiosk and the broken cigarette machine.

"I s'pose you two think you're funny?" I snapped, once we were back on the road and heading away from the campsite.

"I'm sorry," Kiera smiled, glancing back at me.

"It's like being in the company of Laurel and freaking Hardy," I said.

"Oh quit your complaining," Murphy grunted, tearing at the chocolate bar wrapper with his teeth.

"Hey, that was meant for me," I said, leaning forward in my seat and trying to grab it from Murphy.

"It's mine," Murphy barked, shoving my hand away. "Besides, you didn't want it. If I remember rightly, you threatened to give that poor guy some kind of rectal examination with it!"

"Whatever," I said, slumping back into my seat, listening to Murphy's jaws chomp away at the chocolate.

Kiera looked at me, struggling hard not to laugh. "Oh come on, Mr. Grouch," she smiled. "I thought we were friends again?"

"We are," I winked at her.

"Does that mean I've got to put up with you two wandering around like a couple of loved-up teenagers again?" Murphy groaned.

"I thought you'd be pleased for us," I said.

"I am," Murphy sighed, "But if you think I'm gonna put up with you two listening to all that romantic crap on Kiera's iPod, you've got another think coming."

"We don't listen to romantic crap," I snapped back at him.

"Yeah, you do," Murphy groaned. "So if you think I'm gonna listen to hours and hours of freaking Barry Manilow while you two sit and gaze into each other's eyes, you can forget it."

"I've never listened to Barry Manilow in my life..." I started.

"Don't you lie to me," Murphy shot back, eyeing me in the rearview mirror. "I caught you listening to that song once...what was it called? *How am I supposed to live without you?* That was it."

"That's sung by Michael Bolton, not Barry..." I started.

"It's all the same to me," Murphy cut in. "And besides, how do you know all this stuff? You're meant to be some blood-sucking creature from below ground. Instead, you spend your time wandering around with your thumb up your arse, listening to songs written for girls."

86

Kiera started to laugh.

"What's so funny?" I asked her with a frown.

"Nothing," she said.

And although I knew it was me Kiera was laughing at, I didn't care. I was just glad to see her looking happy again. I hoped it would last. I hoped she was wrong about being led down a dead end.

Chapter Seventeen

Kiera

I dozed in and out of sleep as Murphy steered the car high up into the Cumbrian Mountains. Sensing that our journey was nearing its end, I wanted to try and get as much rest as possible. Now that Potter and I had made our peace, my whole being felt more at ease with itself. Had I done the right thing by giving myself to Potter again? I didn't know, and somewhere deep inside of me, I no longer cared. If what the Elders said was true, and I wouldn't be going back with my friends, then I wanted to love and be loved by the man who made me happy while I still had the chance. Potter said we would stay together. He said that was his choice to make, but I wasn't so sure about that.

With my head resting against the window, I peered through my half-open eyes and down at the landscape stretched below. The sun was setting in the distance, and the white fields looked trapped between a thin strip of bright gold. Streams snaked their way through narrow gorges way below. The fresh stream water bubbled and twinkled in the fading light. For the first time in ages, I felt an immense sense of calmness wash over me. I closed my eyes and slept again.

Potter shook me gently awake. I rubbed sleep from my eyes with the backs of my hands. It was dark outside. I peered through the windscreen, trying to get my bearings.

"We're here," Potter said in a hushed tone.

"The Dead Waters?" I asked, my voice still sounding sleepy. I stretched my legs straight in the foot well of the car and yawned.

"The forests surrounding them," Potter said, pushing open the back door and stepping out.

I shoved against the door with my shoulder and climbed from the car. The night air was cold and crisp. It pinched the end of my nose. I looked up, the sky was black and star-shot. A full moon hung in the sky. It was bright white, with a blue haze shimmering around it. I couldn't ever quite remember seeing such a full moon. It was perfectly clear and seemed so close I could reach up and touch its cratered surface. Murphy was standing in his carpet slippers by the edge of what was known as the secret forest. In the moonlight, I couldn't help but notice how drawn and tired he looked. A length of his silver hair had flopped over his right eye. He thumbed it away. I remembered the story he had told me about his life and I wondered if he was standing in the spot where he had said goodbye to Pen as a boy. Had this been the place they'd shared their first kiss? I wondered.

The fir trees stretched high above us, tall and black in the night. They grew close together like an impenetrable wall, barring our entry into the forest. It was as if the trees were keeping the forest's secrets safe. The forest had plenty of them. This was the place I had been born. My real mother, Kathy Seth, had given birth to me here as my father had looked on in terror. The forest is where Murphy had snatched up my body and ran to the Dead Waters – the place he dared to try and hide my lifeless body.

With Potter following close behind me, I approached Murphy.

"Ready?" he asked.

"Yes," I nodded, taking a deep breath.

"Let's not waste any more time then," Murphy said, glancing back over his shoulder as if we might have been followed here by someone. He grunted, faced front, and set off into the forest.

I grabbed his arm. He stopped, a questioning look etched on his face.

"Before we reach the Dead Waters, will you take me somewhere?" I asked him.

"Where?" he asked.

"To the place I was born," I whispered.

Murphy looked into my eyes as if searching them somehow. "Okay," he whispered back, then set off again.

With Potter at my side, we followed Murphy as he cut his way through the trees. There was no path, no marks or signs to lead us in the right direction. None of us spoke. The only sound was that of our shallow breathing. For some reason, and I couldn't be sure why, my stomach had tied itself into a nervous knot. It felt hard and uncomfortable. Was I scared about what lay ahead? If so, why? I had been here before. Before the world had been *pushed,* I'd been led here by Murphy – just like now. He had come because he had made a deal with the wolves – but they had set him a trap. My brother Jack had trapped him. Why had Murphy always been so ready to trust the Lycanthrope, whereas Potter had always hated them? Was it because Murphy had loved a wolf? Was it because I was a half and half? Perhaps he had always been so willing to trust the Lycanthrope because he needed to. It, in some way, justified the choices he had made in the past when it had come to certain Lycanthrope in his life – half and half's like me, or full-bloodied Lycanthrope like his beloved Pen? I couldn't be sure.

We had been walking sometime in the light of the moon that cut between the branches of the trees in thin silver slices, when Murphy suddenly stopped. He looked at me and said in a whispered voice, "This is the place, Kiera. This is where you were born."

I looked about, my eyes as keen as ever in the dark. I don't know what I'd been expecting, but it looked like any other part of the forest. "How can you be sure this is the right place?" I asked. "It was over twenty years ago."

"I will never forget that night, Kiera," he said softly. "Your mother was propped against that tree over there." Murphy pointed to a large Spruce with a moss-covered trunk.

I stepped away from Murphy and Potter and made my way slowly towards the tree. I tried to picture my mother there, but it was impossible. I had never seen a picture of her – I only had to go on what Jack had told me. She had long, thick, black hair like mine, with pale skin and hazel eyes.

"What was my real mother like?" I asked without turning to face Murphy.

"You look a lot like her," Murphy said, staying back with Potter.

"I meant, what was she like as a person?" I asked again. "Jack told me she was evil. He said she was a killer."

"He told you the truth," Murphy said.

To hear it from Murphy made my stomach clench. I now understood why I had felt so fearful on my way here. I was scared I had been born from a ruthless killer. A child killer, just how Jack had described her.

"So she killed children then?" I whispered.

"She was a wolf, Kiera," Murphy said, his voice soft. "That's what wolves do."

"And Pen?" I asked, looking back over my shoulder. "Did she kill children, too?"

"No," Murphy said sombrely, with a shake of his head.

"Why not?" I pushed for an answer.

"Because she refused to give in to the curse," he explained.

"So my mother had a choice then?" I asked.

"We all have a choice with how we live our lives," Murphy said, Potter standing silently beside him.

"So why did my father love her then?" I shot back.

"That was *his* choice," Murphy said. "Like I said, Kiera, we all have choices. Some we regret more than others."

"And what was your choice that night?" I asked, my bright hazel eyes fixed on his.

"To leave you to die or save you," he said straight back.

"And do you regret the choice you made?" I whispered.

"Never," he said.

"Even though I was born from a wolf...a child killer?" I asked.

"None of us ask to be born," Murphy said. "None of us choose our parents. But we can choose not to be like them, Kiera. I know that's what you fear. You fear you might become like your mother – you might turn out like your brother, Jack. Just because you are part wolf doesn't mean you have to be like one of them. You can choose to be nothing like them – you can choose to be better than them."

I looked back at the tree where my mother had pushed me into the world. I'd had two mothers in my life and both had made bad choices. Both had given in to a curse. Kathy Seth, the lust for killing, and Jessica Hudson, the craving for the red stuff. Murphy was right; I hadn't chosen either of them. But I did have a choice now, and I chose not to be like either of them. I just wanted to be me – Kiera Hudson.

Slowly, I turned away from the spot where I had been born. "I've seen enough. Let's get going," I said without looking at either Murphy or Potter. Silently, the three of us set off in the direction of the red lake, which we had come to know as the Dead Waters.

Chapter Eighteen

Kiera

The moon seemed brighter than ever as we reached the lake. Its waters sloshed against the shore in crimson waves. Sand covered my boots like freckles as I stood on the shore and looked across the Dead Waters. It stretched away before me, the trees surrounding the other side looking like a vast black shadow. The lake stretched away for as far as I could see to my right. To my left, and although I couldn't see it, I could hear the thunderous roar of the Fountain of Souls as it raced upwards into the night sky, carrying the souls of those the Lycanthrope had slaughtered since time had begun. Hidden behind the fountain were the caves where the Lycanthrope lived. Sam had said they were deserted now – that the wolves had gone to Wasp Water – but were there some wolves still hiding out behind the fountains?

White shards of moonlight reflected off the red water like broken slithers of glass. Apart from the distant roar of the fountain, this world hidden behind the trees was deathly quiet. Potter and Murphy stood on either side of me. Both of them looked at me, as if I knew what to do next. Knowing that time was short, and we had yet to find Kayla and Sam, I looked down at my hands. The blood I had sucked from Potter's neck was already losing its power. The backs of my hands, wrists, and forearms were once again covered. Just as before, a fine, white dust seeped from the ragged cracks. My skin felt taut, my arms growing heavy.

Slowly, I hunkered down and traced my fingertips over the surface of the red water. At once I felt the strangest of sensations. It was like my fingers were sucking up the red water, like they had become straws. I watched the skin turn supple again as far as my knuckles. Seeing this, I plunged both my hands beneath the water. It was cold, and my fingers tingled. I pulled my hands from the lake. Holding them up before me, I inspected them in the moonlight. The cracks had faded.

Standing, I started to undress. Looking at both Murphy and Potter, I said, "Look away."

"Even me?" Potter asked.

"Definitely you!" I shot back.

Murphy turned his back to me without any hesitation, while Potter lingered.

"Turn around," I hissed.

"But..." Potter started.

"Just turn around, you freaking weirdo," Murphy barked at him. "We haven't come here for you to get your rocks off. Pervert!"

"I'm not a pervert," Potter started to argue, turning his back to me.

I stripped down to my panties and stepped into the water. With my arms crisscrossed over my breasts, I looked back at Potter and Murphy and said, "What are you waiting for? Get in."

They stripped naked. The white light from the moon made their bodies look as if they had been carved from alabaster. I looked at Murphy's naked body and could see a network of cracks spreading out from the centre of his firm chest like a spider's web. Some were deeper than others, but each of them bled a white dust-like powder down the length of his stomach. Potter's body looked the same, although his flesh, unlike Murphy's, was fractured around his well-rounded shoulders and down his back.

I turned away from them. The water rippled around my ankles, calf muscles, then thighs as I headed out deeper into the lake. I looked over my shoulder to see Potter and Murphy coming towards me. When the water was deep enough to cover my breasts, I stopped and waited for them to join me. Standing in a small circle, we looked at each other as the red water lapped against our pale flesh.

"So what happens now?" Potter asked.

Before I'd had the chance to answer, I suddenly started to feel warmer. At first I couldn't be sure if it was the temperature of the water which had changed, or my skin. The water fell suddenly still, not even a ripple broke the surface. I looked past Murphy and Potter. The lake now looked like a vast, red-tinted mirror. I began to feel warmer still and I looked at my friends, realising that the heat was, in fact, coming from my core somehow. It was like my soul was being awakened.

"Can you feel that?" Murphy whispered, his silver hair gleaming beneath the moonlight.

"Yes..." I started then grabbed my own chest, suddenly lurching forward in the water. The red waters splashed up, some of it going into my mouth. It tasted not like fresh spring water, but of blood. It was hot in my mouth, and warmed the back of my throat as I swallowed.

"What's wrong?" Potter asked, as I steadied myself, still holding my chest beneath the water.

"It feels like..." Before I could finish, I bolted forward again, as if shoved violently from behind. I felt something I hadn't felt since before waking up on the mortuary slab. It felt like my heart was struggling to start beating again.

"My heart..." I gasped, pressing the palms of my hands between my breasts.

Murphy and Potter glanced at each other, then they, too, shot forward. Each grabbed their own chest, shaking violently as if receiving electric shocks from a defibrillator. I shook all over as my heart started to race again. It was a feeling I had forgotten, but welcomed. My heart raced like a trip hammer inside of me. I could hear it in my ears. I could feel the blood surging through me again.

"My heart is racing," I gasped. "My heart is beating again!"

"Mine too," Potter said, as if trying to catch his breath.

"It hurts," Murphy cried.

"You're probably having a fucking heart attack, you old fart," Potter said, steadying his friend.

"The pain is going," Murphy wheezed, straightening up.

"What does this mean?" Potter said, the water now lapping beneath his chin.

"One thing is for sure," I breathed, "we aren't dead anymore. It's like the water has brought us back to life."

I lifted my arms from beneath the water and studied my hands. The skin covering them was pearly white and just as smooth looking. I had never seen my skin looking so healthy and clear.

"But I thought these were called the Dead Waters..." Potter started but broke off suddenly. He twisted his head to the right, then quickly to the left. He made a snarling noise in the back of his throat. It echoed back off the surrounding trees like thunder. Potter's face started to change. His nose turned up, his ears stretched into points on either side of his face. Black hair bristled from every part of his body as he started to thrash about in the water. His wings sprung from his back, sending up waves of bright red water. It was then I remembered seeing such a creature before. I had seen Luke look like this once, as he sat hidden away in the forbidden wing. I was seeing Potter as his true self – in his true Vampyrus form. With his body covered in gleaming black fur, and his face contorted beyond recognition, Potter truly did look like a vampire bat. He rolled back his head, his wings beating rapidly, spraying water across the lake, where it fell from the sky like rain. Then he was gone, soaring high up into the night sky. I looked at Murphy, and just like Potter had, he began to change into his true Vampyrus form. Clawing at the air with his fists, I watched his hands stretch out of shape. His spine made a popping sound as his wings shot from his back. He twisted and turned in the water as his body oozed lengths of silver hair from beneath his skin. Just like Luke hadn't scared me, neither did Potter and Murphy. In a perverse kind of way, they looked beautiful – like no other creature seen before. It was like the Dead Waters had truly brought them back to life again.

Then as Murphy blasted up into the night, I started to change, too. Just like I had back in the cramped bathroom in the caravan, I changed into my true form. As I wasn't a true Vampyrus, I was spared the bristling hair and the whole pointy ears thing. But there was something different now. It was like the Dead Waters were fully drawing the true me to the surface. It was bringing both sides out – the Vampyrus and the Lycanthrope. Jack had said I'd always had keen sight because of the wolf that had been hiding inside of me. Now just as the waters were red, so was my sight. The whole world appeared to seethe around me. It looked as if it were on fire. I could see the slightest movement in the trees, each leaf moving in slow motion. I looked back towards the shore and could see individual grains of sand, each one as clear as a shiny new pearl. I looked up at the stars, and each one of them seemed to shoot across the night sky like a blazing meteorite. I'd never seen the world in such clarity before. It didn't matter in which direction I looked, my eyes would zoom in – focus on the smallest of details. I saw a bird darting from the treeline. As I watched it soar just inches above the surface of the lake, the bird seemed to slow down so I could absorb every detail. I could see each individual feather ruffled by the breeze. I looked away, then blinked. The redness had gone. The world no longer looked as if it were on fire. My eyesight, as keen as ever, no longer showed the detail I had seen just moments before. Would it return? I didn't know.

I looked up to see Potter and Murphy swoop out of the sky, heading back towards the lake. They dive-bombed beneath the surface and disappeared from view. I stood in the water, the sudden waves created by my friends' impact breaking over me. I rubbed the water from my eyes to see Potter and Murphy reappear from beneath the water. Both looked like my old friends again.

"What happened?" Potter choked, spluttering water from his throat.

"I dunno," Murphy coughed.

"I think the water has made us whole again," I breathed. "I think it brought out what we truly are. I think it has cured us of our hunger for the red stuff and restored our skin."

"And what about them?" Potter said.

"Who's them?" Murphy asked.

"Them!" Potter breathed, pointing back towards the shore.

Together, Murphy and I looked in the direction Potter was pointing.

"I knew it," Murphy whispered to himself. "I knew it."

"Knew what?" I breathed, looking at the statues which had gathered on the shore.

"I knew they were following us," Murphy said, heading back across the lake towards them.

Chapter Nineteen

Kiera

Potter threw my shirt at me from the shore. I snatched it out of the air. With it trailing in the water, I put it on. With one eye on the statues that had suddenly gathered along the shoreline, I pulled on the rest of my clothes and boots. They stood, grey and lifeless, their heads and hands tilted up towards the night sky. All of them were young – no older than sixteen or seventeen years in age. I counted eight in all. Potter glanced at me as he pulled on his coat, then back at Murphy, who was passing amongst the statues. Buttoning up his shirt, Murphy stopped before one of them. With his nose just inches from it, he stared into the statue's upturned face. Taking a deep breath, I made my way along the shore to where Murphy stood, seemingly transfixed by the statue. Then, so quick that if I'd blinked I would have missed it, the statue suddenly moved. It lowered its face and held out its hand. Swinging from the statue's fist was Murphy's crucifix. Covering my open mouth with my hands, I realised this was the statue of the girl I had seen moving about the grounds of Hallowed Manor. Just like before, her face was a network of ancient-looking cracks and fractures. Her eyes were two white spheres.

With my newfound heart starting to race in my chest, I stopped just inches from Murphy and the statue of the young girl. Potter joined me.

"Meren?" Murphy whispered, screwing up his eyes and inspecting the statue, who now looked blankly back at him. "Is it really you?"

Slowly, he reached out and took the crucifix from the statue's cracked hand. He looked in awe at it, then back at the statue.

"Sarge?" Potter whispered. "Is that Meren? Is that your daughter?"

"Help me," Murphy barked, taking hold of the stone girl before him. "Help me get her into the Dead Waters."

Potter went to the statue, placed his arms around the back of her and heaved. "Fuck, she's a heavy girl," he wheezed.

Murphy shot him a look.

"Sorry," Potter muttered and doubled his efforts.

"Let me help," I said, wrapping my arms around the statue's legs.

"On three," Murphy grunted, bending his legs at the knees. "One...two...three...*lift!*"

Together we heaved the statue off the sandy shore and struggled with her towards the water. With the red waves lapping about our boots like blood, we dropped the statue into the water. A wave splashed up high above our heads. The statue rolled over, then disappeared beneath the water. I stepped back onto the shore, as Murphy stood knee-deep in the water.

"Did she sink?" Potter whispered from beside me.

"Shhh," I hushed back, unable to take my eyes from the water where the statue had disappeared.

Suddenly, a flurry of red bubbles appeared on the surface of the water. Murphy staggered backwards. The water continued to bubble like a saucepan of boiling hot water on a stove. Without warning, something broke through the surface and shot at speed up into the night sky. At once, the three of us snapped our heads back to see what had suddenly appeared from beneath the Dead Waters. High up in the sky I could see something dark corkscrew at speed through the bright moonlight. At first it looked like an arrow, but as I peered up through the night, I saw two black wings unfurl on either side of it. Red water sprayed from them, raining down on us like tears. The water splashed our upturned faces, as the figure swept about.

"Meren?" Murphy breathed out loud.

I looked up again and as the figure swept out of the sky, I could now clearly see it was indeed a young girl. She fluttered left, then right, swooped and soared. To watch her reminded me of the time I had secretly watched Kayla in the grounds of Hallowed Manner as she had taught herself how to fly. Although this young girl was the same age as Kayla – sixteen or seventeen – her hair was blue, not red like my friend's.

She swept gracefully out of the sky, her wings beating softly like that of a giant butterfly. The black surface of her wings twinkled in the moonlight as if encrusted with a million diamonds. Gently, she landed on the shore, white sand seeping between her toes.

"Meren?" Murphy croaked. I glanced at him to see tears glistening on each cheek. "Is it really you?"

"Dad," Meren smiled at him. And when she smiled, her whole face seemed to blossom. Her bright hazel eyes blazed a fiery orange. Unable to hold back any longer, she raced across the shore towards her father, white dress whispering around her calves. Her dark blue hair flew out behind her like streaks of lightning. She was truly beautiful.

Murphy closed the gap between them in three giant strides, snatching her up in his arms and spinning her around and around, her feet lifting off the shore. Meren's wings made a humming sound over the noise of Murphy sobbing.

"Meren, Meren, Meren!" he cried. "My precious daughter. Oh, my God, sweet Meren you have come back to me."

"I love you, Dad," Meren cried, tears now streaming down her face.

With a lump in my throat, and with my eyes starting to sting, I glanced at Potter to see silent tears rolling down either side of his face.

"Are you okay?" I whispered, reaching out and gently squeezing his hand in mine.

"I know how much that means to my friend," he said. "All I ever wanted was to see him happy – or as happy as an old fart like him can get."

"You really care about him, don't you?" I whispered.

"He's been like a father to me," Potter said, watching Murphy and Meren cradle each other. "And now I have a sister, too."

I turned to look at Murphy and Meren. "And I have a cousin," I whispered.

"She looks like you," Potter said, sliding his arm about my shoulder and holding me close. "Beautiful."

We watched as Murphy held his daughter at arm's length, as if studying her. And although his face was streaked with tears, he had the widest smile I'd ever seen spread across his face. "I've never seen you look so well before," he beamed. Then glancing over his shoulder at us, he added excitedly. "The Dead Waters have cured her. They have given her life. She is no longer sick, weak, and fragile. She's like you, Kiera." Then, as if being struck across the face, he looked at me and I knew what he was thinking.

"The Dead Waters," I gasped. "That was the difference between me and your daughters and those other children hidden away at Hallowed Manor. That's why I flourished and they didn't. You placed me in the Dead Waters just moments after I was born. It was the water – the souls of those murdered by the Lycanthrope – which gave me my strength."

"So, just like they have cured us of our cravings – made our hearts start to beat again, they have saved Meren and..." Potter started.

Before Potter had the chance to finish, Murphy was darting between the other statues and shouting, "Where is Nessa? We must get Nessa into the Dead Waters, too!"

"Dad," Meren whispered, the smile she once had, now fading. "Dad, Nessa didn't make it."

"What are you saying?" Murphy said, glancing back at her.

Meren went to him, took him in her arms and said, "She faded away, disintegrated into dust before we got here. Many of us woke a few weeks ago from our graves at Hallowed Manor. Why we had come back, we didn't know. But we quickly turned to stone, some of us quicker than others. I came in search of you – I knew you would be able to help us. But our journey has been a difficult one, only being able to move if we came into contact with blood. Peter went in search of Lot-13 in the Manor House."

"Peter?" Murphy quizzed with a frown.

"Do you remember the other two children in the hospital?" Meren asked him. "They were brother and sister – Alice and Peter?"

Murphy nodded as he remembered, and I remembered them too. They had been weak, almost lifeless, their bodies translucent as they lay hidden in the attic at Hallowed Manor. It was then I remembered the dream I had about a boy crawling towards me and asking for his sister, Alice. They had been trying to reach us – ask us for help.

"Peter managed to get into Hallowed Manor, but it was difficult for him. He could barely move as he was more stone than flesh," Meren continued. "But he came across a boy sleeping in a bed, so he fed just a little from him, but he was disturbed by..."

"By Kayla," Potter suddenly cut in. "Peter was the statue Kayla saw standing at the foot of Sam's bed as he wrestled with the change the matching had brought upon him."

"We were around you all the time," Meren said, looking at me.

"I'm sorry," I whispered, feeling as if in some way we had ignored their pleas for help. "Like you, we had only just woken up in this *pushed* world. Until now, we never truly understood what or who you were."

"To be honest," Potter said, "I thought you were just another part of this fucked up world. Just another piece in the Elders' sick and twisted game they've been playing with us."

"I'm sorry we let you, your friends, and Nessa down," I said, my heart beginning to ache for them.

"You were turning to stone, too, weren't you?" Meren said, looking at me.

"Yes," I whispered.

"That's why we followed you this far," she said. "You seemed to know more than we did somehow. I believed you could help us."

"I saw you – I saw all of you at so many different times," I said, remembering.

"It's a bit difficult to hide when you're made from stone, you kinda stick out a bit," Meren smiled, and yes, Potter was right, she was truly beautiful. "But you left a trail of blood behind from the many fights you fought – and that's what kept us going. Especially you," she said, turning her attention to Potter. Those police officers – the wolves beat you bad and you bled into the snow. That helped us move on."

"I'm glad I was of service to you," Potter muttered, taking a cigarette and popping it into the corner of his mouth.

"I remember looking up and seeing the statues – you – as I was shoved into the back of that police van."

"All of you left so much blood," Meren said. Then, looking at me, she added, "The half-eaten rats in the graveyard..."

"Rats!" Potter grimaced through a cloud of smoke at me.

"I was turning into stone, too, I took anything I could get," I said.

"We took them, too," Meren smiled at me. "But for some of us, the little bits you left behind weren't enough, and they faded away to dust." Meren looked at Murphy and added, "It wasn't enough for Nessa, and I lost her. I'm so sorry, Dad."

"You have nothing to be sorry for," Murphy said, taking his daughter in his arms again. "I believed I had lost both of you, I had come to terms with that. Never in my wildest dreams did I think I would ever have this opportunity to feel such happiness again. To have one of my precious daughters with me fills my heart with such happiness that I don't want it to be touched by the smallest flicker of sorrow." Murphy lent forward and kissed his daughter tenderly on the forehead. "Let's get the rest of your friends into the waters."

Together the four of us lifted the other statues into the water. As we waited silently on the shore for them to surface, I glanced at Murphy and Meren. I remembered the statues I had seen in the graveyard – the statues the Elders had shown me. The statue of Murphy had been with two females, both I had believed were his daughters. But Nessa wasn't coming back, so who was the other? I wondered.

Chapter Twenty

Potter

Just like Murphy's daughter had, the statues we placed in the lake caused the water to rise up, froth, then bubble. The red water suddenly began to violently stir, then erupt as the remaining statues shot out of the water and raced up into the night. Their silhouettes glided over the moon, as they spread their wings. Now that they were free, they whisked through the night, I understood that sense of freedom they must all now be feeling. To fly, to soar, to swoop and dive was a feeling like no other. It was freedom. To look down upon the Earth from such heights gave you a detached feeling – a sense that you were not a part of the real world, just a spectator, watching the world pass by below. Those freed statues would be feeling all of that now. And like me they would remember those feelings – that sense of freedom – for the rest of their lives.

One by one, they swept out of the sky and landed on the shore before us. Their wings buzzed, hummed, and fluttered behind each of them. All of them were female, apart from one.

"This is Peter," Meren said, introducing him to Murphy.

"Good to meet you," Murphy said, pumping the boy's hand up and down.

"Thank you," Peter said politely.

I got the sense he was still unsure of what had truly just happened to him. As far as I could understand, the boy had spent his entire life hidden away in the attic at Hallowed Manor. He had been murdered by Luke and Sparky, only to have come back to life again as a statue in a world that had been *pushed* out of place. Fuck me – no wonder he looked so bewildered and lost.

"This is my twin sister, Alice," Peter said, ushering a meek-looking girl to the foreground. Just like her brother, Alice had light blonde hair, which was long and curly. Both had hazel eyes, which were bright and keen. In fact, as I looked at the gathering of teenagers, I noticed all of them had eyes just like Kiera. All must have been half and half's, just like her.

"Good to meet you," Murphy smiled at the girl.

"Hello, she said, just above a whisper.

Sensing their unease, Murphy hooked a thumb in my direction and said, "This is Potter. He is a Vampyrus, just like me." Then, looking at Kiera, he added, "And this is Kiera. She is a half and half, just like you."

A soft murmur went through the small gathering of half and half's as they all turned to look at her. I could see Kiera looked embarrassed at the sudden attention.

"Hi," Kiera smiled back at them.

The others looked back at her in awe. They had followed her this far after all.

"Why were you not in that hospital with us?" one of the female half and half's suddenly asked. Her voice was soft.

"I was never ill like you," Kiera started to explain. "I am like you, though. I am half Vampyrus, half Lycanthrope, a half and half. But unlike you, soon after I was born, I was placed into these waters and they made me strong. Just like they've helped me, these waters have now helped you. You will no longer be fragile, weak, and ill. You will no longer need the red stuff to stop you from turning to stone. You will be the people you were born to be."

"I feel my heart beating," Peter smiled, pressing his hand against his chest.

"I feel mine beating too," Kiera smiled back at him.

"I've never felt so hungry," Alice said.

And she wasn't the only one. Since being *pushed* back into this world, I had lost my appetite. Other than blood, food had just become a tasteless mush, but now, as I stood on the shore, my stomach ached not for blood, but food. Knowing that Kiera and Murphy had plenty to discuss with the others, I wondered what more I could bring to the party.

"How about I go and find us something all to eat?" I asked. "I'm sure I'll be able to find something."

"I could come with you?" Kiera said, looking over at me.

"No, it's okay," I smiled. "You stay. It looks like you've got a lot of explaining to do. I'll be back real soon."

Kiera stepped away from the others and came towards me. Slowly, she raised her hand and pressed it flat against my chest. "Your heart is beating too," she smiled up me. Her skin looked radiant, her hair almost glowing in the moonlight. "It's beating fast."

"It always used to around you," I said, gently placing my hand over her heart. I could feel it gently thumping away.

"Are you all right?" Kiera frowned. "You look like you've got something on your mind. I thought you'd be glad to be alive again."

"I'm worried about Murphy," I said.

"Murphy?" Kiera asked. "But why? He has his daughter back."

"That's what bothers me," I said, glancing over my shoulder at where Murphy stood with Meren and the others.

"I'm not sure what you mean?" Kiera frowned at me again.

"You said at the end, when we *push* the world back, we go back to where we came from, right?" I said, looking into her eyes.

"Right," she said.

"Well, Meren is dead back there, so is Murphy," I breathed. "We're all dead back in that world."

"But the Elders showed me Murphy and Meren..." Kiera started.

"The Elders showed you statues, Kiera," I said. "They showed you *statues*."

"So what are you saying?" Kiera asked, looking suddenly sad and deflated again.

"I'm not sure," I said thoughtfully. "But we both know statues definitely don't have freaking heartbeats."

I turned to walk away, and as I did, I heard Kiera say, "See you later alligator."

Looking back one last time, I smiled and said, "In a while crocodile."

I didn't want to piss all over her happiness – that was the last thing I wanted to do. At first I'd been just as happy as she had been on seeing Murphy reunited with Meren again. But if we did *push* the world back like we were planning on doing somehow, would Murphy lose Meren all over again? Would I lose Murphy all over again? What were any of us going back to? We were all dead back there. Kiera said she was the only one who couldn't go back. She saw that as a punishment, but was it? Perhaps it was her gift for finally making her choice. Perhaps Kiera was the only one who was going to survive this?

I took another smoke from my pocket. Lighting it, I headed back into the forest that surrounded the lake, in search of food. I hadn't gone very far, when I saw movement to my left. I snapped my head around, fangs and claws out in an instant. Movement to my right this time. I span around to find a figure hidden by shadows between the tree trunks.

"Who's there?" I snarled, bearing my fangs.

"Shhh," the figure said, stepping from the shadows. "It's me, Kayla."

"Kayla?" I breathed on seeing her come towards me. "Where's Sam?"

I didn't even hear her answer. The back of my head exploded in pain, and my world went black.

Chapter Twenty-One

Kiera

Murphy built a fire so we could cook whatever culinary delights Potter managed to find in the forest. Potter had brought back road-kill once, before the world had been *pushed*, and had tried to kid us all that he had hunted the muntjac down. But Isidor had spotted the tyre tracks imbedded into the dead animal's bloodied fur. Potter scowled at him and they didn't speak for a day or two after that. Luckily, there weren't too many roads around here, so whatever Potter brought back would have to be fairly fresh.

As Murphy lit the pile of sticks and branches he had collected from the forest, I sat with the others on the shore by the fire. The moon had started to dip in the sky and I guessed that dawn was no more than a couple of hours away. The Dead Waters continued to lap the shore in red waves, and in the distance I could hear the fountain thundering its way back up into heaven – if such a place existed.

"What's that noise?" Alice asked, scraping her long blond hair behind her ears with her fingers.

"The Fountain of Souls," I told her. It felt odd to be telling her such a thing. It didn't seem that long ago that I had been here with Potter, Murphy, Isidor, and Luke. It was I who was then learning about this secret place hidden in the forest. "It's believed that the fountain runs upwards, carrying souls back into heaven."

"Souls?" Peter asked, crossing his legs as he sat next to his sister.

"The souls of all those the Lycanthrope have murdered," I continued to explain. "A lot of them would have been children."

"Why children?" Meren asked. "That's a bit creepy, isn't it?"

"Yes," I said.

"So the water is red because of all the blood that has been shed," Meren said, looking thoughtfully at the waves which crawled up the shore towards her. "The Lycanthrope took lives, but the water is somehow giving it back, right?"

"Right," I said as she turned to look at me. I could tell that Meren was a quick thinker and nobody's fool.

"But we're all half wolves, aren't we?" another girl in the group asked.

"What's your name?" I asked her.

"Gayle," she smiled.

"Yes, Gayle, we are all half wolves," I said. Then, glancing up at Murphy as he dropped another armload of sticks onto the fire, I added, "but we don't have to be like them. Every one of us here has a choice to make."

"What's that?" asked Peter.

"We choose how we wish to lead our lives," I said, looking at the group before me. "You can make your lives wonderful – make them count. Or you can choose a different path, like those wolves who decided to take the lives of others. That isn't a life – that's an existence. Forever looking over your shoulder, waiting for the Vampyrus to catch up with you."

"But apart from my dad and his friend, Potter, there are no other Vampyrus here," Meren said, as if in deep thought. "There are no more Vampyrus to police them. The Lycanthrope are the police here. So, who then will stop the wolves from killing?"

"Us," I said, looking at the group.

"But there is only a handful of us," Gayle spoke up. "We can never defeat the wolves."

"Not on our own we can't," I said. "But *together* we can. Together we can do anything – if we're determined enough. Maybe that's why the Elders forbid mixing between the Vampyrus and the Lycanthrope. Perhaps they feared what we would become. If we choose wisely, we can become the best of the Vampyrus and wolves. Like wolves, we have great sight, we are loyal to our own kind, our jaws have an incredible crushing pressure when we bite..."

"But doesn't our enemy have these exact same traits too?" A girl sitting near the back of the group spoke up.

"You're right. They have those skills too – but do they have a set of these?" I half-smiled, releasing my fearsome claws. "Not only can we swipe, slash, and rip, but they are also pretty neat at causing some serious blunt force trauma. You should see the damage my friend Potter can do with his fists when he gets going." Then, glancing at Meren, I added, "Your father is pretty handy too."

Meren smiled back at me.

"Unlike the wolves, we can move at incredible speeds," I said, then flashed amongst them in a fleeting spray of shadows, so as to prove my point.

"I've heard that in some parts, that's called *blinking*," Gayle said.

"I like that," I smiled back at her. "Okay so we can *blink* but we can also do this!"

With a quick and sudden shake of my shoulders, I released my wings and shot into the air. I hovered above them, those claws at each tip snatching at the air. "We own the skies; the wolves don't," I said.

"So we can escape quicker than the wolves," Alice said.

"No," I said. "Any army that controls the skies wins the war. We can look down upon them. We can see where the wolves are. Where they are heading, how big their number is, and we can strike from above before they even know we are there. And with our ability to *blink,* we can change our formation instantly. The wolves won't know which way to turn. They won't know from which way our attack will come."

"You make it sound like we are going to war," Peter said, looking up at me hovering above their heads.

"Not war," I said, dropping slowly out of the sky and settling on the shore again. "An *intervention*."

"What's that?" Alice asked.

"This world has been *pushed*," I started to explain. "This world is run by wolves. They have overrun the humans and bent them to their will. They are matching with human children and are slowly destroying them. If we do nothing, then the humans will no longer exist. In the world I grew up in – the world I came from – that was called genocide."

"What do we care for the humans?" another of the half and half's spoke up.

"Do you not care that human children are taken from their parents, driven out in the night and held captive in prisons masquerading as schools? Does it not frighten you that these children are chosen to be matched with wolves, and those that aren't are sent back to their homes, towns and villages, turned dumb so that they cannot speak of the horrors they have seen? If we stand back and do nothing – regardless of the fact we are not humans – then we may as well join the wolves. Because to sit back and do nothing, is as bad as taking part. But each and every one of us gathered here now are only able to do so because of the blood that has been shed by the humans. If it wasn't for the blood spilt into these Dead Waters – then we would be dead also. We are not human; you are right about that, but the best part of me – the part I cherish the most – is my humanity. The ability to love and be loved – to offer kindness and understanding – those are the things I want to define me. All those qualities make us different from those wolves. And I believe we are different because we have been bathed in the Dead Waters. We have the humans to thank for being different to the other wolves. I am proud to be different from the rest. We owe the humans that at least. I, for one, cannot sit on my hands and do nothing – I have to intervene. I have to *push* back."

"I can't sit back and do nothing either," Meren said, getting up and coming to stand shoulder to shoulder with me.

I looked at the group, and out of the corner of my eye, I saw Murphy watching me.

"I want to push back, too," Peter said, standing up.

"Me too," Alice said, joining him.

One by one, the others got to their feet. And it was as I looked at them all staring back at me, I realised they were looking at me expectantly, as if waiting for me to say something more.

"I don't know about you guys, but I'm starving," I smiled back at them.

Chapter Twenty-Two

Potter

I opened my eyes and went to put a hand to my head, but I couldn't. My hands were secured behind me. I twisted my wrists and heard the sound of metal chains clinking. I was lying down on my side. The ground was hard, made of stone and covered with straw. It was something you would find a wild animal caged in. The cell stank of piss and shit. I tried to lift my head off the ground to get my bearings. The back of my head throbbed from where I'd been struck. The cell was dimly lit and something about it seemed familiar, but I just couldn't be sure where I'd seen it before. Slowly, gritting my teeth against the pain, I lifted my head. There was a cell door. The hatch was open and a stream of white light poured in from whatever lay on the other side.

I slowly turned around on the floor. There was a small bed, the type you get in a police station cell. It was a hard plinth of concrete. Placed on top was a plastic-looking mattress. It looked more comfortable than the floor. Despite having my hands cuffed behind my back, I would have struggled up onto the bed if it hadn't already been occupied. I could see the shape of someone lying on it.

"Hello?" I croaked. My throat felt dry and sore. "Hello?" I managed again, wondering if I was sharing the filthy cell with another prisoner.

The shape rolled over, then swung its feet over the side of the bed.

"Hello again," a voice said. It was soft and female.

Straining, I lifted my head an inch off the ground to try and see who the voice belonged to. My new heart leapt at the sight of Kayla looking down at me from the bed.

"Kayla?" I gasped. "They got you, too?"

"No, I'm one of them," she said.

"Look, this isn't the time to start throwing one of your fucking hissy fits," I groaned. "Just get down here and untie me."

"You don't understand," Kayla said, standing up. "I really am one of *them*."

"What the fuck are you talking about?" I muttered, twisting my wrists in their chains. "Where's Sam? Maybe I'll get some sense out of him? Doubtful – but you never know."

"Sam?" Kayla said, screwing up her nose. "Who's Sam?"

I looked at her standing above me, bright flaming red hair and brilliant yellow eyes. "You really aren't Kayla, are you?"

"No," she smiled. Then, shaking herself free of Kayla's skin, she revealed the wolf hiding beneath.

"A fucking wolf," I groaned. "I might have guessed. When am I ever gonna learn my lesson not to trust a bit of skirt?"

"Potter," the wolf said, licking its snout with a huge pink tongue. "Oh, Potter."

"Who are you?" I sneered.

The wolf padded towards me on its giant paws. It was covered in a coat of gleaming white fur. A bushy tail wagged excitedly out behind it. I remembered how Murphy had described Pen. Was this her?

"Pen?" I whispered.

The wolf cocked its head to one side. "Lola," the wolf eventually woofed.

Lola? My mind scrambled through the pain. Lola? Hadn't Sam mentioned a wolf named Lola? Hadn't this wolf wanted to match with Kayla?

With my heart starting to race, I stared into the wolf's piercing yellow eyes and said, "What have you done with Kayla? Where is she?"

"We thought you might be able to tell us that," the wolf barked.

"Who's *we*?" I shot back.

Before Lola had a chance to answer, the cell door was swung slowly open. A stream of fluorescent light spilled into the cell, momentarily blinding me. With my eyes screwed half shut, I peered up at the figure looming in the doorway.

"Who's there?" I snapped.

My question was answered with a soft, wicked chuckle. The figure stepped out of the blinding light and into the cell.

"Hello, Potter," Jack Seth smiled, his bright orange eyes spinning wildly in his emaciated face. "How is my little sister, Kiera?"

Chapter Twenty-Three

Kiera

Potter had been gone some time – too long to search for some food. Leaving Murphy with the others, I set off up the shore to look for him. I followed his footprints, until they led away from the sand and into the forest. With the trees seeming to close in all around me, I headed into the gloom. With my eyes seeing through the darkness, I was easily able to follow the marks he had left behind. The broken twigs and disturbed undergrowth were all obvious pointers to the direction in which he had travelled. I made my way amongst the overbearing tree trunks until I came upon an area where the ground had been almost trodden flat. Hunkering down, I inspected the ground. The area hadn't been trodden down, like I had first thought. Somebody had fallen to the ground here. Potter? I wondered.

Brushing my fingers delicately over the ground, I came across two other sets of footprints. One set was definitely that of a female, and the other, a tall male. Crouching, I edged my way around the track marks, looking for the direction in which they had headed. There was no sign of Potter's footprints, so I could only assume he had been carried away over the shoulder of the male. The male's footprints were deeper on his route away from the scene than they were on his approach, telling me he had carried something heavy away with him. Fearing that something terrible had happened to Potter, I jumped to my feet and started off after the footprints. They led away from the direction of the lake and out of the forest. Why would anyone come to take Potter? My mind scrambled. Had whoever taken him come across him by chance? Had he been taken by wolves? Skin-walkers? We had been told by Sam that the wolves no longer lived near the forest, they had all vacated the caves behind the Fountain of Souls and were now in Wasp Water with the Wolf Man. Had Sam got it wrong or had he *lied*?

There was nothing here for the wolves anymore. There was only the lake...

"The lake," I breathed out loud, stopping in my tracks.

The wolves might not live here anymore, but what if they knew the power of the Dead Waters? Hadn't Sam told Murphy that the wolves wouldn't want us coming to the lake because of the waters' healing properties? So why then leave them unguarded....?

"It's a trap!" I gasped. "We've been led into a trap."

If they had taken Potter already, what about Murphy and...

"...the half and half's..." I breathed, then suddenly I dropped to my knees. Blood trickled from my left eye. This was something which hadn't happened for a while. Had my body been too much like stone before – unable to shed any blood, needing every last drop? Whatever the reason, it now dribbled from my eye and onto my cheek. Then, just like a flashbulb going off in my head I saw Jack Seth again. Those flashbulbs had been away for too long. Had bathing in the Dead Waters restored that inner ability to be able to *see*?

Jack was standing on that stage again. A sea of body parts whizzed over my head and clattered into him. The crowd roared and it was deafening. I clapped my hands to each side of my head and covered my ears.

Traitor! Traitor! Traitor! The Skin-walkers roared at him.

But who had Jack betrayed? The wolves? But he was one of them.

Who did you betray, Jack? I screamed at him over the roar of the crowd. Who did you betray?

You, little sister! he smiled back at me. *I betrayed you and your friends. I betrayed all of you!*

"No!" I cried out, those flashbulbs fading in my mind. Wiping away the blood from my face with my fingertips, I clambered to my feet again.

Spinning round, I raced back the way I had come, back towards the lake and the others. With my hair streaming out behind me, I clenched my teeth and....*blinked*...as Gayle had called it. The world became a blur around me as I raced through the trees. Each trunk passed me like a fleeting shadow. I broke through the treeline and onto the shore. Snapping my head left, I could see my friends gathered around the fire someway off along the shore. Then, snapping my head to the right, I saw a throng of wolves silently making their way towards them. They approached with their heads down and bellies almost dragging along in the sand. Their tails protruded like arrows from behind them. Their bodies looked sleek, huge, and powerful beneath the dying moon.

Turning my back on them, I raced along the shore towards Murphy and the others. Within seconds, I had reached them.

"We've got company," I said to Murphy, jabbing my finger in the direction of the approaching wolves.

Jumping to his slippered feet, Murphy barked, "Where's Potter?"

"They've taken him already," I said, eyes wide.

"Then it's just me and you," he said, unbuttoning his shirt.

"And the others," I said, glancing at the group gathered around the fire.

"We can't expect them to fight," Murphy growled at me. "They're not used to dealing with shit like this."

"We've got to learn to defend ourselves sometime," Meren said, springing to her feet.

"And now looks like a good time to start," I said, the wolves now picking up speed and racing along the shore towards us.

"Up! On your feet!" Meren shouted at the others still gathered by the fire.

True to their earlier promise, all of them sprang to their feet.

Realising he was never going to talk Meren or any of the others into backing down, Murphy looked at them and barked, "Form a line!"

Without question, they stood up along the shore.

"Wings," Murphy snapped as the wolves bounded towards us. There was a thunderous beating sound as we all released our wings.

"Hold the line!" Murphy ordered.

The wolves were so close now, that we could see the drool spraying from their giant foaming jaws. I glanced to my left at Meren. Her claws and fangs were already out and gleaming brightly. Her hair shone an electric blue.

"Hold," Murphy whispered. "Just a few more seconds."

The wolves were almost on top of us now as they bounded at a terrifying speed towards us. Sand sprayed up from beneath their vicious-looking paws, and their eyes shone so bright, the light which seeped from them was almost blinding.

"Now!" Murphy roared, shooting up into the air.

We followed his lead and leapt into the night, the wolves missing us by inches below. Some of them skidded to a halt in the sand. Others yelped and growled, craning their giant heads up to see where we had suddenly disappeared to.

"Now let's kill the fuckers!" Murphy roared, plummeting out of the sky and onto his prey.

Within an instant, Murphy had snatched one of the wolves off the shore and was slicing and dicing it into quarters with his claws. Entrails and fur-covered lumps of flesh rained out of the black sky as Murphy shredded the wolf. As if spurred on by this, the others dropped out of the sky. With their claws and fangs at the ready, they bit, clawed, and ripped at the wolves below. The wolves fought back, lunging up at the approaching half and half's with their mighty paws and cavernous jaws. But we were faster – slicker. And just like Gayle had said, we *blinked* at speed around the wolves. They spun around as if chasing their own long bushy tails as we *blinked* before them, above them, behind them, to the side of them, all at once. We raked at them with our claws, slicing open their thick throats in violent sprays of black blood. I saw Peter zoom forward, his wings arched high behind him. With his mouth open, he ripped into the snout of a wolf. Then, soaring upwards, he took half of the wolf's face with him. It dangled wetly from his mouth, then he spat it out. Peter wiped the blood away, then dropped out of the sky once again to finish off the wolf, which now lumbered blindly around on the shoreline.

I looked down at the sand, which was now covered with so much blood, that for a moment, I thought the lake had completely washed over the shore. Meren raced out of the sky, her claws out before her. In the light of the moon they glistened like a set of blades. A wolf lunged up at Alice as she swooped through the air. Unbeknown to the wolf, Meren was approaching on him fast. Just as the wolf's mighty paw was about to knock Alice out of the air, Meren had sliced open its back and was soaring away with its spine dangling from her claws. The wolf collapsed into the sand like a pile of fur-covered jelly.

Behind me I heard screaming. Spinning around in the air, I saw a wolf standing up on its back legs. Its jaws were fixed tight around the ankle of one of the girls. She beat her wings furiously as she desperately fought to stay airborne. The wolf was strong, heavy, and he was yanking her back down towards the ground. With the claws opening and closing on each of my wings, I raced forwards, the wind rippling against my face. Dropping low so my stomach was just millimetres above the sand, I raced towards the wolf. With my arms tucked in against my sides to give me as much speed and propulsion as possible, I rocketed towards the wolf that had now almost pulled the girl out of the sky.

As I skimmed past, the claws at the tips of my wings sliced through the back legs of the wolf. With a bewildering yelp, it released its crushing bite on the girl and collapsed. She shot free into the sky, blood trailing from her mauled ankle. The wolf tried to stand, but without any back legs, it rolled over onto its side, where it lay panting, its giant tongue lolling from its wide jaws. Spiralling upwards, I back-flipped, and then raced towards the ground. With my lips pulled back and fangs out, I tore the wolf's head free from its neck. Fur and blood oozed between my fangs. I let the wolf's head fall from my mouth and into the Dead Waters, where I spat a wad of fur and blood from my mouth. With my wings thrumming as fast as my heart, I hovered in the sky and surveyed the carnage below me. The shore was littered with disregarded wolf body parts. The last of them were losing their fight with two of the half and half's.

Murphy swooped in and hovered beside me. He grunted with satisfaction at the sight below him.

"They did good," Murphy said. Then, looking at me, he added, "Now we go and get Potter, Kayla, and Sam back from whoever has them. And when we find out who has our friends, we rip him a new arsehole, right?"

"Right," I said.

Murphy then swooped away from me, and back towards the shore.

Chapter Twenty-Four

Potter

"I might have known you'd be behind this," I said, Seth dragging me to my feet. "And to think that Kiera nearly had me believing that there was a chance there might be some good in you."

"She told you about me then?" Seth asked, shoving me towards the open cell doorway. "She told you I was her brother?"

"Yeah, she did," I spat. "I think she took the news quite well, considering."

"Considering what?" he asked.

"If I'd found out I was even remotely related to you, I would've slit my own fucking throat," I sneered at him.

"Nice," Seth said, forcing me out of the cell.

I staggered into a narrow corridor and finally realised where I was being held. It was the police station in Wasp Water. I'd had a row with Kiera in this cell block. Although she would never have admitted it, she had been jealous over Eloisa. She'd had no reason to be. Eloisa had been a lying, cheating, murdering wolf.

Lola's paws click-clacked over the stone corridor as she sauntered along beside me and Jack. Just like my cell, the whole place stank of piss and shit. But then it would, wouldn't it? The place was overrun with wolves.

"So where are you taking me?" I asked Seth, as he led me out of the cell block and through the police station. My hands were still secured behind my back.

"You'll soon find out," Jack said.

"So what have you done with Kayla and Sam?" I hissed.

"Nothing," Seth smiled at me.

"Don't fucking lie, the wolf looked like Kayla," I said.

"Lola can shape-shift, just like me," Jack explained.

"Stop treating me like a retard, Seth," I groaned. "I know the wolf would need a drop of Kayla's blood to shift like her. Just like you needed some of McCain's back at Ravenwood School."

"I matched with her once," Lola barked. "Not completely, but enough so as I can shift to look like her."

"I couldn't give a monkey's toss if you matched with her or not," I said, stumbling forward up the narrow corridor. "But I promise you, if either of you have so much as harmed one single hair on Kayla's head, I'm gonna rip your fucking lungs out."

"More threats you can't possibly keep," Seth smiled, his thin lips twisting in a crescent moon shape.

"I'm guessing you're the brains behind this whole thing. You're the person they call Wolf Man, aren't you?"

"Me?" Jack laughed. "Not me, Potter. I'm not the Wolf Man."

Lola made a woofing noise beside me as if she, too, were amused by what I'd said.

"So who is then?" I asked as Seth pushed me up a spiralling staircase. We stopped outside a wide wooden door.

"You mean you haven't figured it all out yet?" Seth grinned. "You mean Kiera hasn't been able to *see* who it is?"

"Leave Kiera out of this," I said, reaching the top of the stairs.

"I plan to," he said, his eyes bright and boring into mine. "But the Wolf Man has a different plan altogether."

"Well why don't you just take me to this Wolf and let me..." I started, then stopped as Seth pushed open the door before us to reveal a room. There was a desk with someone sitting behind it.

"Hello, my old friend," the man behind the desk said. "It's good to see you again."

"Luke?" I whispered, as Seth closed the door behind us.

Chapter Twenty-Five

Potter

"You!" I roared. "You're this Wolf Man? It's been you the whole time!" Despite having my arms secured at my back, I lunged across the table at him. "You're not even a fucking wolf!"

Seth took hold of me, and placing his hands on my shoulders, he forced me down onto a chair at the opposite side of the table from Luke.

"Still the hothead," Luke said, his bright blue eyes twinkling back at me. "And as for not being a wolf, the wolves just want to be led. After all, you've tried to dominate them for two lifetimes and you're a Vampyrus, just like me. But unlike you, Murphy, and the Black Coats, I've given the wolves their freedom."

Luke looked just as I remembered him to be, his thick black hair was swept back off his brow, the lower half of his face was covered in a black shadow of stubble, the deep cleft in his chin looking like a puncture mark. He wore a white shirt open at the throat and faded blue jeans.

"You were meant to be my friend!" I bellowed at him. "You were meant to be Murphy's friend, Kiera's friend. We trusted you."

"No, it was I who trusted you," Luke said softly. "It was you who betrayed me."

"Betrayed you?" I couldn't believe what I was hearing. "How did I betray you?"

"You knew I was in love with Kiera, but you took her for yourself," he said.

"So that's what this is all about?" I stammered. "Because you lost the girl to me?"

"Not just any girl," Luke said matter-of-factly. "A rather special girl, as you have probably now discovered."

"Kiera has always been special to me," I barked at him.

"Touching," Luke smiled, getting up from his seat. The office was small, and lit with a lamp on the desk. Blinds had been pulled down at the windows, and I couldn't tell if it were day or night outside.

"So why have you come back?" I asked. "I thought you were dead."

"I wouldn't have had to come back if you hadn't have ruined my plans," Luke said. "If you had just left me and Kiera alone, none of us would've died, I would be ruling the world that we had once known..."

"And we would've all lived happily ever after," I smiled at him. "What a load of old bollocks. You just wanted to use Kiera. You only wanted her to love you so when it came to Kiera making her choice between the humans and the Vampyrus, she would've chosen the Vampyrus. She would have chosen you."

"And would that have been so bad?" Luke snapped. For the first time since entering the room, Luke now sounded rattled. He was starting to get angry. "The Vampyrus could have ruled the Earth."

"No, *you* would have ruled the Earth," I cut in.

"With Kiera at my side," he said. "I would have made her a queen. What have you made her?"

"Happy," I smiled.

Springing from the table, Luke smashed his fist into the side of my head. I flew from the chair and onto the floor. Fuck, that really hurt! Seth hoisted me back onto the chair. With the side of my head feeling as if it had been struck by a train, I raised my head in defiance and looked Luke in the eyes.

"You will never ever get Kiera to be with you," I whispered.

"I wouldn't be so sure about that," Luke said.

"Kiera is in love with me," I said. "You'll never get her to look twice at you with me in her life."

"Exactly," Luke said. "That's why you're going to have to die. And then I will slowly take those who mean anything to her and kill them. In the end, she will be begging to get into bed with me to save those she loves. I already have Kayla," he smiled.

I looked into his eyes, and I wasn't sure that he did have Kayla. If he did, then Luke would have already used her as pawn in his sick game. He wouldn't have been using this wolf Lola to masquerade as her. He was bluffing. I didn't know where Kayla was, but something was telling me that Luke didn't know either.

"If Kiera won't marry me, perhaps Kayla will," Luke smiled. "After all, I got her to fall in love with me once before. And boy was she sweet."

"You fucking pervert," I spat at him.

"Fucking Kayla, that's what I'll be doing," Luke grinned at me. "I'm sure Kiera will happily swap places to save her friend." Then, leaning in close so our cheeks were almost touching, Luke whispered in my eyes, "It's a shame you won't be around, I could have invited you to our wedding. You could have been my best man. I might have even let you *watch*."

The thought of Luke with Kiera made my stomach knot. Hot bile rushed up into my mouth, and my heart raced. If only I could get my hands free.

"Tell me, Potter, is Kiera a *screamer*?" Luke laughed in my ear.

I couldn't listen to him anymore, so snapping my face quickly to the right, I smashed the side of my head into his. Luke staggered sideways, clutching his head in his hands. A thin line of blood trickled from his ear.

Luke twisted his head to look at me, and I could see the hate in his eyes. He wanted to kill me.

"If you want to kill me, why don't you just do it right now!" I roared at him. "Go on, kill me while I'm chained up. That's what a coward like you would do."

Rubbing the side of his face with his hand, Luke forced a smile and said, "This place is way too private. I want your execution to be very public. I want everyone to see what I do to people who betray me. I want everyone to know what I do to traitors. I want Kiera to understand my threats aren't idle. Jack could have taken her as simply as he took you. But I want Kiera to come to me. I want her to come into this town, crawling on her hands and knees, begging me to make her my queen. Only then will I know she is mine."

"She'll never be yours," I said stubbornly.

"It's a shame you won't be around to see how wrong you are," Luke said, heading for the door. "But perhaps in another time – in another when – you'll see."

Keeping my head held high, wanting to show him he could never beat me, Luke stared at me from the doorway. I looked at him with utter defiance.

Turning to look at both Seth and Lola, Luke said, "Get his execution ready. I want him dead already."

Without another word, Luke left the room, leaving me alone with Lola and Jack Seth.

133

Chapter Twenty-Six

Kiera

We swooped over the hills and mountains in the direction of Wasp Water. Murphy took the lead. No longer fearing that we might turn to stone at any time and drop from the sky, we raced towards Wasp Water. Although Murphy's sole purpose for heading straight there was to rescue Potter, in the back of my mind, I had another reason, too. In my recent nightmares, I had seen Jack Seth being executed in the town square. He had been accused of being a traitor. But I had seen him in those flashbulbs inside my mind. He had confessed to setting a trap for me and my friends. Which premonition was true? I sensed that I would find out in the town of Wasp Water.

We flew side by side, me and the others stretched out across the sky. The mountain peaks whisked past below us, and just like in my nightmare, they were covered in snow. The sun was peeking over the top of them, making the snow look orange in places. The air was crisp, and the membrane covering my wings rippled like washing hanging out to dry.

With the town of Wasp Water looking like a faint smudge in the distance, we swept towards it. Believing we had almost reached Wasp Water without warning the wolves gathered there, the dawn sky suddenly lit up with gunfire. A girl to my right yelled out in pain as her wings became tattered with holes. She spiralled away towards the ground at great speed, her wings beating uselessly on either side of her. I snatched a glance over my shoulder to see three helicopters sweeping in towards us like giant wasps.

I banked immediately to the left and swooped down, away from the helicopters which were now pursuing us.

"We've got one right behind me," I heard Meren yell.

I twisted around in the air as another helicopter roared past, its rotatory blades a thundering blur. The word POLICE was printed down the side of its black metal body in white letters. Whoever the Wolf Man was, he had anticipated the fact that we would fly into Wasp Water, so he had the skies surrounding it patrolled. I shot forward, then rolled into a three hundred and sixty degree spin. My stomach lurched so violently, I thought for a moment that I was gonna be sick. I was now behind the helicopter which was racing after Meren. A Skin-walker leant from the inside of the machine and fired wildly at her. All around me, I could see the other half and half's and Murphy scatter as the remaining helicopters buzzed after them.

I righted myself in the air, then flew alongside the helicopter. The Skin-walker firing from the side of it had no idea I was there. He wore a black flight suit, with a black helmet and visor. He fired another volley of shots. The bullets thudded into the body of one of the half and half's, who then dropped lifelessly from the sky. Perhaps I had been wrong about us controlling the skies after all. We could easily outrun these helicopters, but what would be the point? They had seen us now. If we brought them down, we might buy ourselves a little more time to get in and out of Wasp Water.

Then over the roar of the rotary blades, I heard Peter shouting triumphantly, "We got one! We got one!" as he yanked one of the armed co-pilots from his seat and tossed him through the air. Alice was holding onto the side of one of the helicopters, her wings just a blur as they flapped behind her. With her claws buried in the side of the machine, she hung from it, as if pulling it out of the sky. The pilot turned the helicopter around in a full circle, as if trying to shake her free. Peter scurried over the front of the thundering wasp, and climbed inside. Blood splattered the front window as Peter removed the pilot's face with his fangs. He leapt free, snatching hold of his sister as the helicopter spun out of control as it raced towards the rocky ground below. It crumpled into a seething ball of flames and black smoke as it collided with the side of a mountain. A cheer went amongst us as we watched it burn.

I heard another volley of gunfire snake across the sky. The co-pilot in the machine I was chasing was firing at Murphy as he soared through the sky towards Meren. Suddenly, Murphy began to plummet out of the sky, holding his side.

"I hit him! I hit him!" I heard the Skin-walker say into his mouthpiece.

Meren raced through the sky after her father.

I banked sharply to the left and swooped round to face the helicopter. The sky pulsated and exploded with colour as gunfire and smoke lit up the dawn. The rotary blades were whizzing around and around like a huge silver spinning top. They spun through the sky as if slicing it open. The helicopter's surface was shiny as glass and lights flashed on its belly. In its smooth black surface I could see my own reflection, my bright yellow eyes and fangs were gleaming back at me as I raced towards it.

I hit the front portion of the machine like an arrow. The glass windshield splintered and the whole helicopter seemed to shudder and vibrate. The blades made a whining sound above me. The giant black wasp-like machine went into a violent tailspin. Seizing the moment, I reached for the co-pilot. With my claws buried in his chest, the black visor covering his face smashed open, revealing a drooling snout.

"Oh no you don't!" I roared over the rushing wind. I couldn't risk the Skin-walker changing into a wolf on me – not hundreds of miles up in the air as I clung to the side of a helicopter. That wasn't good.

With my claws still buried in the Skin-walker's flesh, I shot upwards and away from the helicopter. The creature howled and barked, its helmet splitting in two to reveal its huge skull. I hovered over the spinning blades below and let go of the Skin-walker. He clattered into them. The blades carved through him, shredding him into thin ropey strips which flew away into the air. Entrails became entangled around the blades and the motors that propelled them. They made a *chugging* noise as the helicopter began to lose altitude.

Throwing myself into a nosedive, I raced after it and back towards the ground. As I gathered speed, I felt a crushing feeling against my chest and my cheeks began to pull tight across my face under the sheer swiftness of my decent. My wings had tucked themselves in against my body, so I tore through the sky like a bullet.

I'm gonna have to pull up! I yelled inside, the ground racing up to meet me.

Hold her steady, I told myself, drawing level with the cockpit.

Another rapid volley of gunfire tore all around me.

Reaching into the cockpit, I ripped open the throat of the pilot as he shouted frantic messages, I guessed, back to the police station control room in Wasp Water.

With the Skin-walker spraying blood from his throat, I pulled up sharply, soaring upwards. My wings fanned out on either side of me, as I flew just a few feet above the fields below. I felt a blast of heat wash over me as the helicopter exploded just below.

I raced back towards my friends. Meren was racing through the air, her father in her arms. I could see the blood pumping through his fingers which were clutched to his side.

There was one helicopter remaining, picking off the half and half's. I scanned the sky and could only see Alice, Peter, and Gayle left flying. I followed their blazing wings as they raced towards the helicopter. Gritting my teeth, I pushed forward. Coming up behind the machine, I roared around and tore after it, as the co-pilot released another volley of gunfire.

"Peter, its right behind us!" Alice yelled, her eyes bulging with fear.

Perhaps Murphy had been right. Maybe these half and half's weren't ready to fight yet. They didn't seem able to move with speed and agility as other Vampyruses. But then it had taken me time to learn how to master the art of flying.

"Try and shake it off," Gayle hollered.

"I can't," Alice screamed, as the co-pilot fired at will again.

I rolled sharply to the right, then to the left, dodging the gunfire as I raced through the sky towards the helicopter. My wings beat powerfully up and down, their claws snatching at the air.

"I can't shake him!" Alice screamed as the helicopter thundered after her.

Wave after wave of gunfire lit up the morning sky, as I lurched from side to side and up and down.

"Alice, he's right on you!" Gayle hollered.

The helicopter hovered right behind Alice.

I looked to the left and could see the pilot sitting in his cockpit. He turned to face me and raised the visor on his helmet. His eyes burnt red and orange in their sockets.

Then over the sound of the roaring helicopter, I heard someone yell, "Form up on my right! Form up!"

I looked back over my shoulder to see Murphy and Meren racing through the sky towards us. Murphy still had one hand pressed against his side.

"I've been hit! I've been hit!" I heard Alice scream as she fluttered away, her wings in tatters.

Murphy swooped alongside me, as did Gayle, while Peter shot through the sky after his plummeting sister. "We've lost too many out here!" Murphy roared at me. "We can't afford to lose one more."

Together, the four of us raced after the helicopter. Reaching its tail, we split, Murphy and Meren one side, me and Gayle the other. Reaching out with our claws, we took hold. Like black-winged locusts, we scurried over the helicopter and towards the cockpit. The pilot lurched the machine violently left then right trying to shake us free. My stomach flipped over. Murphy went to work on the other side of the helicopter, removing large pieces of the machine with his claws. The engine made a whining sound as I reached the cockpit. With one quick swipe of my arm, I reached inside, yanking the co-pilot from his seat. I threw him screaming into the air. Gayle plucked him out of the sky with her claws. She shook him all over as she tore the Skin-walker in two. Both parts of him span away towards the ground, entrails fluttering like kite tails.

Then out the corner of my eye, I saw the cockpit window blow inwards. I snapped my head to the side to see Meren shove her face through the opening she had made with her claw. Snapping wildly with her fangs, she lunged at the pilot's throat. With blood spraying from her mouth, she threw her head backwards, ripping the pilot's windpipe free. She spat it out and wiped her lips with the back of one claw.

"Done?" I asked her.

"Done," she grinned.

"Let's get out of here then," I smiled back at her.

We fluttered away as the helicopter spiralled out of control towards the uneven and rocky ground below.

Chapter Twenty-Seven

Potter

Luke had been gone just moments before several of the Skin-walker cops entered the room. I stood up, but one of them forced me back into my seat with a rough pair of hands. Surprisingly, Seth took a seat beside me. I glanced right at Jack. He sat staring ahead with his bright eyes, and his expression was unreadable – blank.

I looked back at the cops. There were four of them. Snapping her head forward, Lola barked at them as if prompting them to speak.

One of the cops was holding a clipboard. He stepped forward, and looking at me, he said, "You have been found guilty of murder."

"Murder?" I laughed. "I haven't murdered anyone. I haven't even had a trial."

From the clipboard, the cop took what looked like a piece of paper and placed it on the table before me. I glanced down at it. It was a photograph of me holding the dead wolf boy in the barn.

"It is forbidden for a human to take the life of a wolf," he said.

"I ain't no human," I smiled, glancing at Seth. I had him to thank for setting me up so that photograph could be taken.

"You are also convicted for being a traitor..." the cop continued.

"Yeah, yeah, I've heard it before," I said, trying to sound my most cocky and arrogant, but deep in my heart, I didn't have a clue as to how I was going to get myself out of this mess.

I glanced at Seth again. He stared ahead, and for once,

his eyes looked black and dead. The light had gone out of them. Quicker than I believed a Lycanthrope could move, Seth had got up, the flesh from his arms had gone and two meaty, fur-covered claws were raised before him.

The cops looked at one another, then realising they were in trouble, two of them ran at him. I watched as Seth sliced his claws through the air, tearing open the cops' faces. Fur oozed from between the red openings as they threw their hands to their faces and howled. The remaining two cops leapt at Seth and I watched in amazement at what I saw unfolding around me. Seth opened them up so quickly that if I'd blinked, I would have missed all the fun. The skinwalking cops dropped to the floor where they kicked and thrashed, clutching the bleeding wounds Seth had opened in them. As they fought for their lives, the human skins they had stolen fell away, and I looked in disgust at their faces, which now lay bare. The cops' heads were misshapen – elongated – and they each had a criss-cross of open wounds weaved about their skull. Their mouths were huge and gaping, made of long fleshy lips that flapped in and out like giant gills. Wispy lengths of wolf hair hung from them.

Even I turned away in disgust as one of the dying Skin-walkers turned on one of his own and began to devour him. The sound of slurping and breaking bones was disgusting, and if my hands weren't secured behind me, I would have covered my ears.

The door to the room crashed open and a fresh batch of Skin-walkers burst in. Seth turned to face them, his claws held above his head. He snarled, his thin twisted lips recoiling to reveal his pointed teeth. Seth moved towards the cops with such speed, that he had cut through four of them before they'd a chance to fire guns, which they held in their hands. The others came at him, the sound of their breathing deep and rasping as they started to change shape. One of them managed to release off a volley of bullets, and the room flashed bright white. Seth fell to the floor. At first I believed he had been shot. Then spinning on his back like an upturned turtle, he swiped away at the legs of the cops and brought them crashing to the floor. No sooner had he knocked them over, he was up again, leaping through the air at the remaining cops.

I saw it coming but was powerless to act, as I was still manacled at the rear. Lola bounded into the air, colliding with Seth and slamming him into the wall. Seth looked at her, and not for one moment did he show any sense of feeling or pain – his face was expressionless. He then ripped open her throat with his teeth. Lola made a whimpering noise as she kicked out with her back legs and thrashed her tail from side to side. Eventually she fell still, dropping to the floor in a pile of white fur. I looked up at Seth and he looked back at me.

He rushed towards me. But instead of killing me, as I believed he would, Seth reached behind me, and broke my chains free. Jumping to my feet I looked in his eyes, which were now blazing again.

"Why have you saved me?" I asked, rubbing my wrists.

"I didn't do it for you, I did it for my sister," he said, his face wrinkled and hollow-looking. "I did it for Kiera."

"Why?" I asked.

"I thought Bishop was going to kill you," he said, his eyes still fixed on mine. "I had no idea he was going to use you as bait to trap my sister. I might be a sick fuck, but not so sick I'd let my own sister be taken to bed against her will by that freaking bat."

"She got to you, didn't she?" I said softly. "Kiera got under your skin."

"She taught me I have a choice, and I haven't been able to stop thinking about that since I left her in that room," he explained. "For once I want to do the right thing – by Kiera, at least."

"So what now?" I asked, still not entirely sure if *I* could trust him.

"We go to Kiera and stop her from coming to Wasp Water and entering Bishop's trap," Seth said, turning towards the door.

He stopped suddenly.

"What do we have here?" Luke said, standing in the open doorway. "Two traitors! Why, this just keeps getting better and better."

A sea of Skin-walkers stood behind him. Our only way out was blocked.

Smiling, Luke stared back at us and said, "Looks like we're gonna have ourselves two executions today."

Chapter Twenty-Eight

Kiera

With smoke and debris pouring up into the air from the downed helicopters, it was only a matter of time before the good townsfolk from Wasp Water came to investigate. It wouldn't take Einstein to figure out what happened out here. We had to keep moving – get in and out of Wasp Water before we were discovered. But that would be easier said than done. It was a safe bet that if Potter were being held in Wasp Water, it would at the police station, in the cells where I had slept in a world not to dissimilar to this one. In that *when*, Wasp Water had been overridden by zombie-like vampires – it was now home to the wolves.

Murphy held his side as he staggered across the rugged moorland towards the town. He had one arm thrown around Meren's shoulder in support. Peter carried his sister, Alice, in his arms. She was unconscious, the side of her head pressed flat against his chest. This was impossible. Our number had been cut in half. Our chances of beating the wolves had been slim at best, now they were something close to zero. Gayle glanced at me, her eyes haunted by what had just happened. Her strawberry blond hair flicked about her shoulders in the wind. Had I'd led the half and half's to their deaths? I feared. Had I filled them with false hope? Had I been wrong to convince them that because we could fly, and wolves couldn't, that we could easily defeat them? I had underestimated the cunning of this Wolf Man – but then there was nothing so cunning as a wolf.

Stopping dead in my tracks beneath a bruised and battered looking sky, I said, "I will go on alone."

"Don't be so stupid," Murphy snapped. He was paler than ever, and despite the cold wind that gnawed at us, his brow was covered with beads of sweat. "You can't go on alone."

"And you can't go on like that," I said, pointing at his bleeding wound.

"It will heal itself, you know it will," he said, doubled over in pain.

"Not for a few hours yet," I warned him. "And we don't have the time." I remembered the nightmare I'd had about Jack, and something inside told me time was running out for him. Potter, too.

"I'll go with you," Meren suddenly said.

"No one is going anywhere," Murphy growled. "We stay together."

I looked at Meren.

"Kiera's right," Meren said, pulling her father tight. "We could go ahead, scope the place out. See how well defended the town is. We could then come back and plan our attack."

It was as if Meren had read my mind – had seen my plan before I'd had the chance to suggest it. Perhaps we just thought alike?

I pointed ahead. "There is an outcrop of rock over there," I said to Murphy. "You could rest there, unseen by anyone who might come out here to discover what happened to those helicopters. Peter and Gayle could stay with you and keep watch while you and Alice get a chance to heal. Neither of you are any good to us at the moment."

Murphy raised his head and looked at me. "You just take a look and come straight back, right?"

"Right," I said. "Me and Meren check the place out, find the safest way into the town, and then come back here for you guys."

"You got two hours," Murphy grumbled. "If you're not back by then, gunshot or no gunshot, I'm coming after you."

"Okay," I breathed in relief that Murphy had agreed to the plan. I looked at Meren and she smiled back at me. She was pleased, too.

Slowly, we crossed the barren-looking moorlands towards the overhang. The landscape looked ancient, prehistoric perhaps? Large jagged lumps of granite rock pierced the ground like black headstones. The wind blew hard between the mountains and over the rolling hills. Our clothes fluttered about us as we pulled them tight. We stepped beneath the overhanging lip of rock. It was dry underneath and shielded from the howling wind. Working together, Meren and I rested Murphy against the far wall of the overhang. He winced and clutched his side. I could see that his fingers were black and crusted with dried blood.

"Are you okay?" I asked.

"Get the hell out of here before I change my mind," he wheezed. "You've got two hours."

"Okay," I said.

Looking at Meren then back at me, Murphy added, "And bring my daughter back safe."

"I can take care of myself," Meren tried to reassure him.

"You don't know the wolves like we do," he grunted and closed his eyes.

Leaving Murphy to rest, I turned to face the others. Gayle was standing just beneath the lip and looking out across the moors, as if on guard. Alice was asleep on the ground, her head resting in Peter's lap. Her wings, which were folded around her, were riddled with gunshot wounds.

"How she doing?" I whispered, not wanting to wake her.

"She doesn't look too good," Peter whispered back, his eyes wide and fearful.

"Just let her rest," I told him. "We half and half's have a knack for healing."

"I hope you're right," he said, looking down at his sister and brushing a stray strand of hair from her feverish brow.

"We'll be back soon," I said.

Meren was standing with Gayle. Both turned to look at me as I approached them. "Ready?" I asked Meren.

She nodded.

Looking at Gayle, I said, "Keep a look out. You should be safe here and we won't be long."

"What should I do if any wolves come?" Gayle asked.

"Fight for your lives," I said, heading out from beneath the overhang.

I didn't mean to sound flippant or cruel, but I was being honest. I was trying to be real.

Chapter Twenty-Nine

Kiera

Using the giant rocks which were scattered across the plain to conceal ourselves, we made our way towards Wasp Water. Meren stayed close to me, crouching when I did, running when I ran, and hiding when I hid. To the east of the town, I remembered the road that I had walked once before with Kayla and Isidor after escaping the zoo. It led into town, but was sheltered on one side by trees. That would be the safest place to head for, in hopes we could get close to the town without being seen.

Cutting across the open plain at speed, I led Meren towards that road. Just like I had remembered it, a wooded area stretched alongside the road, offering us cover. Once amongst the thick trees, I led Meren towards the road. Coming to rest behind a large tree, I peeked around it. I could see the road about ten yards away. The last time I had walked that road, it had been blocked solid with cars. Each one of them had been filled with the dead, those that had been attacked by vampires. I pushed the memory of their bloated and maggot-infested faces from my mind.

Without warning, a police car sped past on the other side of the trees, its emergency lights screaming and flashing. This patrol car was followed by another and then another. They were heading out in the direction of the downed helicopters and to where our friends were hiding.

Meren looked at me. "What now?" she whispered, combing her blue hair behind her ears with her fingers.

"We wait here for those police cars to get well clear. We daren't risk going out onto that road with so many cops about,"

I whispered back. "The town is about a quarter of mile over there. The trees start to thin out just before town, but we can get close enough to take a look."

"Okay," Meren said, crouching down and resting her back against the tree trunk.

Two more police cars raced past, and I slid back behind the tree and out of sight.

As the sound of their sirens began to fade into the distance, Meren looked at me and said, "Who murdered me?"

"Huh?" I said, surprised by her question.

"Who murdered me back at Hallowed Manor, and why?" she asked again.

Settling back against the tree, I said, "A wolf called Sparky and a Vampyrus called Luke Bishop. Sparky was once a friend of mine, and Luke was a friend of your father's."

"So if they were friends, why did they kill me and the others?" she said, her bright eyes fixed on me as if searching for answers.

"Sparky was deceived by Luke," I started to explain. "Luke deceived all of us. His real name was Elias Munn and he was wicked beyond belief. He thought you were half-breeds – Vampyrus born from the mixing of humans and Vampyrus. We all believed that – I thought I was one, too. He wanted to experiment on you, make an army of half-breeds because he thought they had special gifts – powers. He wanted to make an army of half-breeds so he could take over the world. Slowly he was infecting the human race. He and other Vampyruses were feeding off humans, which turns them into vampires. But these vampires were freakish, frenzied, and untameable – like zombies. He wanted an army he could control, so he started to experiment with the half-breeds. But when he discovered how very weak and sick you were, he knew you would've been of no use to him, so he murdered you in your beds. Instead, he kidnapped a healthy half-breed; he kidnapped my friend, Kayla."

Meren sat quietly as if contemplating what I had just told her. After a few short moments, she turned to face me again and said, "Why were we brought back then?"

I thought about this, and shaking my head, I said, "I don't know. The only creatures that really know why are the Elders, and they speak in riddles. But I believe we are getting closer to the answer – closer to the truth."

Again, Meren sat silently as if registering what I had told her. Then, shooting me a sideways glance she said, "Did you know my mother?"

I thought of everything Murphy had told me and how Pen had given her daughters up as babies. She had left them in a box, sick and weak in Murphy's care. He had told Meren her mother had died. He hadn't told either of his daughters about their real mother. Not wanting to lie to Meren, and knowing the truth should come from Murphy, I looked away and said, "I didn't know your mother."

Feeling a little uncomfortable about keeping the truth from Meren, I got up and brushed the damp leaves from the seat of my trousers. There was little snow on the ground beneath the trees, but there was enough to have made the ground damp.

"C'mon," I said, looking down at Meren. "I think the last of those police cars has gone now. We should get closer to the town. We haven't got long before your father comes looking for us."

I set off, keeping back from the road. Meren followed, then caught up with me.

"I saw you in the summerhouse," she suddenly said with a faint smile. "I saw you and that man, Potter."

I felt my cheeks fill with blood, as I remembered looking up and finding a statue looking in at us as Potter and I had made love. "So that was you, was it?"

"I'm sorry," Meren said with a cheeky grin. "If it makes you feel any better, I didn't see much. The windows were so covered with rain, and it was dark inside."

"Wow, that makes me feel a whole lot better," I said, my cheeks still burning red. I looked away.

"Do you love him?" she asked me.

I looked at Meren and said, "Yes, I love him with all my heart. He can be difficult at times – a real pain in the arse – but I love him all the same. I love Potter more than I've ever loved anyone."

"Will you get married?" she pushed.

"He hasn't asked," I said.

"But what if he did?" Meren wouldn't let up.

"Then I would say yes," I said, with a thoughtful smile.

Meren giggled.

"Besides, it will never happen," I said, bending low to avoid a branch.

"How do you know?" she asked.

"Men like Potter don't ask you to marry them," I sighed. "Men like Potter aren't the marrying type. They can't or won't settle down."

"Why?" Meren asked.

Before I'd the chance to answer, there was a sudden noise in the distance. "Shhh!" I said, pressing my finger to my lips.

Cocking my head to one side, I heard the sound of cheering, followed by someone speaking through a loudspeaker. At once my mind flashed with images of my nightmare. In them I could see Jack being forced to crouch down by a man in a black hood. I could see the blade of the guillotine come slicing down.

"Jack?" I breathed aloud.

"Who's Jack?" Meren frowned.

"Jack's my brother, and he is about to be executed," I said, turning on my heels and racing towards the town of Wasp Water.

Chapter Thirty

Kiera

"Where are you going?" Meren called after me.

"I've got to save him," I shouted back over my shoulder, the sound of cheering in the distance growing louder and raucous with every passing moment.

"I didn't know you had a brother," Meren said, catching up with me.

"Neither did I," I shot back, breaking free of the trees and darting out onto the road.

"This isn't safe," Meren suddenly said, grabbing hold of my arm.

"We promised my dad we would only have a scout about – take a look – and then report back."

"But they're gonna execute my brother!" I snapped, yanking my arm free of her grip.

"That town is full of wolves," Meren tried to reason with me. "They'll spot us a mile off, and then it will be us they're executing."

It was hard to argue her point. I had a sudden thought as I remembered my nightmare. "Do we look so different from them? Aren't we half wolf, too? You can tell human from a wolf because of the colour of their eyes. Our eyes are practically the same as theirs. They won't be able to tell the difference – not if we're careful."

Meren looked down the road towards the town, then back at me. "How do you know it's your brother who is going to be executed?"

"I *see* things," I told her. "Meren, you're gonna have to trust me on this."

"But what about my father?" she said. "We made him a promise."

"I understand if you don't want to break that promise, I really do," I told her. "But I have to go and help Jack." Turning away from her, I raced up the road towards the town. I looked back only once to see Meren darting back off the road and into the trees for cover.

Just like I had in my dream, I made my way through the throng of wolves who had crushed themselves in to the town square. I kept my head down, only looking up if I had to. I pulled my coat about my frame, in the hopes that it made me smaller somehow, less visible. The wolves jostled and bustled all around me. They stank of sweat. Straw lined the streets, and the town looked rundown and tired. The Tudor houses looked uncared for and no longer fit for human habitation. Even though these wolves wandered around in human skins, it appeared they were still very much like animals. Dog shit, or was that wolf shit, lay squashed along the cobbled streets. Blood ran along the gutters, where human remains clogged the storm drains.

Skin-walkers, disguised as humans, crowded into the town square. And unlike in my dream, I knew exactly what they had come to see. I understood why an electric current of excitement buzzed through the crowd.

They stared expectantly ahead, their bright yellow eyes set in their sunken sockets. I eased my way through the Skin-walkers, desperate to get nearer to the stage I knew was up ahead, the stage where my brother would be executed if I didn't somehow manage to set him free. But how? There was only me against hundreds and hundreds of wolves. I didn't have time to go back and get my friends. By the time I would return with them, Jack would be dead. And besides, would Murphy risk everything just to save Jack Seth? I doubted it.

The only person who was ever going to save Jack, was me. But how?

I continued to push my way through the crowds, ducking beneath waving arms, and between the bristling bodies of the wolves. Then ahead, I could hear the sound of that man's voice coming through the loudhailer. It sounded mechanical, like a robot from a science fiction film. The Skin-walkers whooped and cheered, punching the air with their fists. They really were animals.

"Welcome to today's executions," he bellowed through the loudhailer. "Do we have a surprise for you all today!"

The crowd roared with an insatiable excitement as they jostled closer towards the stage, all of them wanting a better look at the gruesome event about to be played out before them. I forced my way forward for different reasons than those of the wolves surrounding me. Just like I had seen in my nightmare, the fountain had been reduced to rubble, and in its place had been erected the stage and guillotine. It towered above the stage, looking bigger and more intimidating in the real world. The blade gleamed like diamonds in the morning light. It looked razor-sharp. Wolves pressed up against me, and the atmosphere was suffocating, thick with a palatable excitement.

"Okay, so let's not delay the main event any longer!" the guy yelled through the speaker. "Please welcome to the stage, our executioner!" The crowd exploded in an uproar of cheers and whistles as the hooded man stepped out on top of the stage. He waved back at the
crowd like some kind of celebrity.

"We love you!" a female Skin-walker screamed, waving what looked like an autograph book in the air.

She'll be throwing her panties up onto the stage next, I thought feeling sick to my stomach.

"He loves you, too!" the guy roared through the loudhailer.

The woman screamed, then fainted, the thought of the executioner loving her back just becoming way too much for her. I saw the female Skin-walker sink beneath the crowd, then heard the sound of her bones crunching as the other wolves trampled over her, desperate to get as close to the stage as possible.

"So who are you going to be beheading for us today?" the guy asked the executioner.

"A killer!" the executioner roared at the crowd from beneath his hood. "A killer of wolves!"

The crowd erupted angrily and pressed themselves against the stage. They punched the air with their fists as they hissed and booed.

"Kill him! Kill him! Kill him!" the crowd started to chant.

From the side of the stage another hooded man was shoved forward. I knew who was beneath that hood, and my stomach knotted.

As I had seen before, he staggered blindly across the stage. His arms were secured behind his back with chains. The executioner grabbed him roughly by the arm.

"Unmask him!" someone roared from the crowd.

"Show us the killer's face!" another yelled.

"Unmask him! Unmask him! Unmask him!" the crowd wailed as one.

Just like in my nightmare, the guy with the speaker teased the audience by shouting, "What was that? I can't hear you!"

"UNMASK HIM! UNMASK HIM! UNMASK HIM!" They screamed so loud, it was deafening.

As if sensing that he had brought the crowd close to an orgasmic eruption, the guy with the speaker stepped forward and whipped off the prisoner's hood.

I threw my hands to my face, as Potter looked bleary-eyed at the crowd. His eyes were swollen almost closed, his nose was bent out of shape across his face, and both lips were bloodied and swollen.

"No!" I screamed, desperately forcing my way through the crowd, confused and terrified at the sight of Potter standing beaten and broken on the stage.

"KILL HIM!" the crowd cried.

"No!" I screamed, my pleas drowned out by the crowd as I pushed and shoved my way forward.

I felt a heavy hand fall on my shoulder. With my heart racing I looked back.

"Hey, lady," a giant-sized Skin-walker said, his eyes spinning brightly. "We don't get to rip him up until the executioner has cut off his head. You know the rules."

I looked away in disgust and back at the stage as the first of the bloody missiles was thrown from the crowd. A lump of red flesh slapped against Potter's chest, where it slid down his stomach and onto the stage. As it spattered wetly on the stage, the air above my head became full of human body parts and remains. They rained down on Potter in thick wet chunks. Blood and innards covered him bright red. Potter glanced up at the sky, and I knew what he was looking for. He was looking for me and Murphy. He was looking for us to come and save him like we had so many times before.

As if giving up hope of being rescued this time, he lowered his head.

I pushed forward, the crowd crushing so tightly about me, I couldn't even open my wings to get airborne.

"Potter!" I screamed over the roar of the crowd. "Potter! *It's me, Kiera!*"

He stood with his head cast down, arms tight behind his back, the blobs of flesh and guts continuing to rain down on him.

"*Stop it!*" I screamed, tears streaming from my eyes. "*Don't hurt him!*"

Deaf to my cries, the Skin-walkers continued to roar laughter and cheers as they threw the last of the body parts at Potter. He stood on the stage, his entire face and body dripped red with blood, guts, and body tissue. When the Skin-walkers had run out of human remains to hurl at Potter, the executioner shoved him back across the stage towards the guillotine.

"Off with his head!" a Skin-walker screeched from behind me, enticing the crowd to cheering excitedly again.

"*No!*" I screamed, desperately fighting my way forward. There were so many wolves crushed around me, it was almost impossible to move.

Potter offered no resistance as he was forced by the executioner to kneel down. I inched my way forward, the edge of the stage just feet away now. The executioner forced Potter's head beneath the guillotine.

"Please," I begged, as I continued to push my way forward. "Please don't hurt him." I edged myself closer to the stage. I had to save him. But there were just too many people. I pushed harder. My heart raced and I felt sick.

"Take off his head!" the Skin-walkers whooped and chanted over and over.

I reached the stage.

"*Potter!*" I screamed over the roar of the baying crowd. I reached for him but there was a barrier preventing me getting any closer. I wanted to touch him.

"Potter!" I screamed, my throat raw, tears raining down my face. Suddenly he looked up. Our eyes met.

"I love you," I whispered, reaching desperately for him with my hands.

"I love you, too," he said. "See you later, aliga..."

The last half of his final word was drowned out by the sound of the blade thundering down at speed. Throwing my hands to my face, I watched Potter's head drop into the bucket before him.

"No!" I screamed, my knees buckling beneath me. *"No!"*

An arm suddenly slipped through mine, catching me before I hit the ground. "Come with me before they realise you are not one of them," a soft voice whispered in my ear.

Sobbing uncontrollably, I turned my face to discover Meren holding me in her arms. She had come back for me. "I can't leave him."

"He's gone now," Meren whispered against my wet cheeks. "Come, Kiera, it's not safe for you here now."

I could barely stand. My sudden grief was so strong. The pain was unbearable. It felt like my soul had been ripped out. I just wanted to curl up and die.

"Leave me here," I said, trying to pull free of Meren. "Leave me here to die next to Potter."

"I can't leave you," Meren hushed, coaxing me away from the stage and to safety. "There are others who need your help."

"And who is going to help me now?" I sobbed uncontrollably. "Who is going to help *me* now that the person I loved more than anything has gone?"

I looked back at the stage to see the executioner hand over Potter's headless body to the howling crowd. I turned away, burying my face against Meren. I didn't want to see what they were going to do to it. That was Potter's body. It had been mine to hold and love. Not for them to defile and rip to pieces.

Feeling as if my whole being had been crushed, and unable to control the gut-wrenching sobs that consumed me, Meren led me silently out of the town of Wasp Water. We hadn't gotten very far, when I dropped to my knees.

"Kiera, please, we've got to keep moving," Meren said, tugging at my sleeve.

"I can't go on," I whispered through my tears.

"We haven't got far to go," Meren insisted.

"I didn't mean that. I can't go on losing people I love. I've lost Isidor and now Potter - I've lost everything. I'm done," I said, curling up on the road. "Let the wolves come and find me. Let the Wolf Man kill me."

I closed my eyes and waited for death to come and take my pain away.

'Dead Push'

(Kiera Hudson Series Two)
Book 7
Coming Soon!

Also available by Tim O'Rourke
'Vampire Shift' (Kiera Hudson Series One Book 1)
'Vampire Wake' (Kiera Hudson Series One Book 2)
'Vampire Hunt' (Kiera Hudson Series One Book 3)
'Vampire Breed' Kiera Hudson Series One Book 4)
'Wolf House' (Kiera Hudson Series One Book 4.5)
'Vampire Hollows' (Kiera Hudson Series One Book 5)
'Dead Flesh' (Kiera Hudson Series Two Book 1)
'Dead Night' (Kiera Hudson Series Two Book 1.5)
'Dead Angels' (Kiera Hudson Series Two Book 2)
'Dead Statues' (Kiera Hudson Series Two Book 3)
'Dead Seth' (Kiera Hudson Series Two Book 4)
'Dead Wolf' (Kiera Hudson Series Two Book 5)
'Black Hill Farm' (Book 1)
'Black Hill Farm: Andy's Diary' (Book 1)
'Doorways' (The Doorways Trilogy Book 1)
'The League of Doorways' (The Doorways Trilogy Book 2)
'Vampire Seeker' (Samantha Carter Series Book 1)
'Moonlight' (The Moon Trilogy Book 1)
'Witch' (A Sydney Hart novel) Book 1
'Yellow' (A Sydney Hart Novel) Book 2

You can contact Tim O'Rourke at
www.kierahudson.com
Or by email at kierahudson91@aol.com

Printed in Great Britain
by Amazon